THE HATCHING

A HORROR NOVEL

MARK GILLESPIE

LOOP 1 - GOD ON THE SUBWAY

Clip Zero.

Shaky cam footage of human traffic rushing back and forth along a low-lit subway platform. The traffic moves in both directions, some of it hurrying towards the stairs and exits while the rest of it, including whoever's holding shaky cam, runs deeper inside the station.

A wailing siren in the distance grows louder.

Shaky cam approaches a long line of people, all gathered around what appears to be an empty train. Most of the people on the platform are filming on their phones, thrusting their cameras towards a window on one of the center cars, next to a set of sliding doors.

The police, who haven't yet sealed off the entire station, try to discourage the onlookers from getting too close to the train. But while some people search for another vantage point away from the prying eyes of the law, others resist with force, resulting in several onsite arrests.

A woman is being interviewed nearby. Her name is Clarissa Jackson and as she talks (although it's more like shouting), she's surrounded by TV people and cameras.

CLARISSA JACKSON: Did y'all see what they did here tonight? They shot God.

Clarissa is a tall black woman, dressed in a long coat with baggy pants and old white sneakers.

It's at this point that a voice begins to narrate over the footage. The voice belongs to Kurt Carpenter, one of America's favorite, longstanding news reporters. Carpenter's voiceover however, is not taken from the original broadcast. It was added later on, specifically for the Loop.

KURT CARPENTER: Ladies and gentlemen, you're watching Clip Zero. This footage is now widely believed to be the first documentation of any kind that alludes to our current global crisis. As most of you know, the shooting at 163rd Street Station occurred exactly one week before the dust storms rocked the planet. Is there a connection? We're still not sure. Nobody knows much about the man who died on the train at 163rd Street Station. Was he just another homeless man with mental health problems? Is that why he took the young boy hostage? No ID was found on the body and the man has never been formally identified. What we do know is that his friends, including Clarissa Jackson who you can see here, called him God. It's interesting to note, ladies and gentlemen, that this disturbance on the subway which garnered little attention at the time, has just passed over three hundred million views on YouTube. Let's hear again what Clarissa had to say that night.

CLARISSA JACKSON: (*still talking to a huddle of reporters*). Y'all understand right? They shot God on the subway. Not just anyone, God.

REPORTER: Clarissa, what happened here tonight?

Clarissa's attention drifts over to the section of the train that's currently sealed off by the police.

CLARISSA JACKSON: He was my friend.

REPORTER: Why did your friend take that boy hostage on the train tonight? Why did he put a knife to the boy's throat?

CLARISSA JACKSON: (*turning back to reporters*) He was never going to hurt that boy and you'd know that if you knew God like I knew God. Wasn't even a real knife in his hand. Nothing but a plastic toy, but I bet they didn't tell you that yet. Hmmm?

REPORTER: So why did he – why did God – do it?

CLARISSA JACKSON: God wanted y'all to stop, look and listen. He wanted you to sit up and take notice of what he had to say. He had the gift you know, and after he saw what's coming he wanted y'all to know and get ready and maybe beg for forgiveness before the end. That's why he did it. God couldn't just stand on a soapbox on Wall Street and hope that you'd all stop and listen, right? Who wants to listen to another homeless man preaching the truth to the sleepwalking dead? Would you? Damn it, this was no hostage situation. There were no demands other than the demand to pay attention.

REPORTER: When he didn't release the boy, the police were forced to take action. Whatever this message was Clarissa, was it worth it? Was it worth dying for?

CLARISSA JACKSON: (*Shakes her head*). That boy was never in danger.

REPORTER: Personally, I think it's honorable that you're defending your friend Clarissa but...

CLARISSA JACKSON: You still ain't listening, are you? All you see is a poor black woman defending a poor black man. Give me a break mister. My friend is dead and you still think he's just another bum that hit rock bottom, ain't that right?

Clarissa addresses the cameras directly.

CLARISSA JACKSON: Y'all didn't listen to God tonight but you sure as hell better listen to me. God had the gift, he tried to warn you. He tried to do something good and instead of listening, they killed him. He tried to tell you that he was never going to hurt that boy. Said he just wanted the cameras, but look at how it's turned out. I guess I'm the one appearing on TV in the end. Now y'all better listen to God's message. Something very big and very bad is coming. I know God and God's been agitated for weeks. Having nightmares. I know, I was there. Y'all thought it was going to be okay, didn't you? Well, y'all thought wrong because you see this blood right here on my hands? That's God's blood. Now y'all wanna know something? Wanna know what he said to me before he died in my arms tonight on that train over there?

She leans closer to the camera.

CLARISSA JACKSON: Kill yourself. That's what God said to me and that's what he wanted to say to y'all tonight. Kill yourself folks because there's a hell coming to Earth that you can't even imagine. Better off dead, that's what God said. And he meant it too because I swear, if you catch up with that body bag they just took away and pull back the zipper, you'll see a mighty relieved-looking corpse grinning back at you.

End of Clip Zero.

1

"Five minutes to soundcheck!"

Dani's heart skipped a beat at the sudden announcement. It's happening, she thought, this is really happening.

She turned around on the barstool, waving at Larry, letting him know the message was received and understood. Five minutes, sure thing. No big deal. Five little minutes. As she waved, Dani hoped that Larry couldn't see how anxious she was about something so trivial, something that he probably considered a mundane chore at this point in his career.

Who got nervous for a soundcheck?

Breathe, Dani told herself. Slow and deep, just like you practiced. You got this, you're a Zen monk sitting on the Himalayas and nothing can touch you.

She convinced herself that Larry hadn't noticed her legs shaking. Why would he? He was too busy up there on the stage, adjusting the angle of the microphone that he'd positioned in front of Dani's one-hundred-watt Marshall combo amplifier. If anything, he was the one that looked nervous and sweaty. Maybe it was just the lights.

Dani turned back to the bar. Her older sister, Chiara,

who'd also acknowledged Larry's announcement with a wave, continued to exchange banter with the Academy's resident sound engineer. Larry was also one of her oldest friends from college.

"Hey Larry," Chiara called out. "What's going on with you man? You look like shit."

"Huh?"

"You alright?"

"Can't talk Chiara. Working."

Dani watched as Larry finished up the prep work. He walked over to the edge of the stage and took the three-foot jump down onto the floor. Wiping his forehead dry, he walked towards the double set of stairs that led up to the second floor and the mixing desk.

"Five minutes guys."

"Heard you the first time," Chiara said, smiling.

Dani picked up the bottle of Bud sitting on the countertop in front of her. The glass was cold and slightly damp, which was bliss in this kind of heat. She finished the bottle and slammed it down on the counter.

"Somebody's nervous," Chiara said.

Dani nodded. "Where's Raven? I could use another one."

"No idea," Chiara said, glancing around the first floor in search of the bartender. "Probably touching up her vampire makeup in the john, you know what goths are like. I'll get you another beer sis."

Before Dani could say anything, Chiara was on the other side of the bar and heading straight for the fridge.

Dani laughed at her sister's boldness. "Can we do that? Just take one?"

"What sort of punk rocker are you?" Chiara said, staring through the glass doors and examining the stock. "Hey,

they've got a pretty good supply in here all things considered. What do you want?"

"Maybe we shouldn't be too fussy."

"You're paying *them*," Chiara said, glancing over her
shoulder at Dani. "Remember? You hired this place for your
gig and you're the one putting money in their pockets
regardless if there's a crowd tonight or not. Sure it's a great
venue, at least it was before the shit hit the fan. But right
now? It's taking up space on the street like every other
useless establishment that lacks paying customers. But
when people hear you sing tonight Dani, they're going to
rush through that door and bring their wallets with them.
That's a win for the Academy so the least they can do is
shout us a few beers."

"Yeah I know," Dani said. "But they gave us a crate of
Bud already. It's upstairs in the green room."

"Yeah whatever. They won't miss a couple of beers from
the bar. It's cool, me and Larry go way back."

Chiara pulled out two chilled Heinekens and walked
back to the bar, grinning like a kid who'd just robbed a
candy store and returned back home a sweet-toothed king.
"Bottoms up."

Chiara used the Academy's bottle opener to pry off the
lids. Then she placed the beers on the counter, sliding one
across to her younger sister.

"Cheers."

Dani grabbed the bottle like it was the arm of a
drowning lover. "Thanks."

They sat there drinking for a while, passing time before
the soundcheck. They were on the first floor of the Academy, a
one thousand capacity rock and roll venue in Manhattan, and
one of New York's hippest and filthiest live music spots. And it
was filthy. Dani hadn't realized just how beat up the old place

was until she'd arrived an hour earlier with her guitar, amp and sister in tow. The wooden tables scattered around the edge of the dancefloor were covered in more scars than an old-time gangster. There was amateur graffiti everywhere, printed on the walls, tables and even on the bar, most of it consisting of love hearts and hard-to-read telephone numbers informing patrons where and when they could get a free blowjob.

Dani could still smell the cigarette smoke inside the Academy, even twenty years after the indoor ban had been introduced. That stale odor was trapped inside these four walls, alive in the wooden floors, and like a restless spirit in an old mansion, its presence had seeped into every crack and corner. Some things could never leave.

Dani and Chiara drank their beers in silence, glancing at the big TV screen fixed to the wall. It was a screen that used to broadcast sports in the afternoon, but now the only thing it ever showed was the Loop, which was currently replaying Clip Zero for the millionth time.

Chiara leaned back on the barstool, tilting her head towards the roof.

"LARRY! You up there?"

There was a pause before the answer came back from the second floor.

"Jesus Christ," Larry said. "What is it?"

"Wanna put something else on TV man? Or turn it off? I'm sick to death of the fucking Loop and seeing the same old shit every day."

Larry appeared at the top of the upper staircase, leaning over the railing. Dani hadn't caught the sound engineer's surname at the load in earlier, but she knew he was of East Asian origin. Chinese? Japanese? Korean? Was it rude that she'd missed the name or couldn't remember it? But despite his ethnic background, Larry was a New Yorker through and through, boasting a colorful Brooklyn accent at odds with his Oriental features.

"Did Raven give you guys those beers?"

Chiara nodded. "Sure did."

"*Those* beers?"

"Yeah!"

"I'm serious Chiara," Larry said. "We don't have enough alcohol as it is, which means you can't just help yourself whenever you feel like it."

Chiara pointed at the big screen.

"C'mon man, put something else on will ya? We've all seen these clips a hundred times before and it's driving me crazy. We know the world's fucked. Okay? It's depressing, we get it. Can't we just forget about what's going on outside for today?"

"I like the Loop," Larry said, drying off his forehead with a Kleenex. "Sure it's repetitive, but it's educational. And you gotta watch it over and over again because that's the point. That's how we spot things, pick up on important details that we missed first time around, second time around, third time around."

Chiara nodded sarcastically. "What the hell are you blabbering on about?"

"You only *think* you've heard it all before Chiara, but you haven't. You gotta go full on Sherlock Holmes with this shit on the Loop. You gotta watch every single clip and keep watching it, studying all the facts and figuring out why every detail matters. And it does matter. Do that and it'll come. We'll find out more about the Burn, its origins and why this shitty situation is happening to us."

Chiara glanced at Dani, twirling her finger at the side of

her head in a loco gesture. "C'mon Larry. Just put Netflix on
or something."

"Nope."

"Asshole."

"Keep it up Chiara. Either way, the Loop stays on."

"Whatever," Chiara said, spinning around on the
barstool like a bored kid. "You know what the Loop's good
for Larry? It's a measuring device. When it finally goes
under like all the other channels that's when we'll know
we're screwed big time. When the Loop goes, we go. And if
there's a silver lining to be found at the end of the world, it's
that I won't have to watch that shit again."

Dani pushed the empty Heineken bottle away. She was
drinking fast, but she couldn't help herself. And she wanted
another because the beer didn't seem to be doing anything
to her nerves.

"Let him watch it Chiara."

Chiara glared at the big screen in disgust. "Look at it for
God's sake. It's just a front for skin cream commercials and
beauty products. Everybody knows they keep the Loop
running, playing the same old crap, just so they can keep
the commercials going and make a few bucks. Sorry folks,
we've canceled all your favorite shows but here are more
commercials in between a bunch of recycled news clips. I'm
telling you Dani, those marketing assholes are harder to kill
than John McClane."

Dani was only half-listening to her sister. She was
looking over the rim of her glasses, staring at her reflection
in the mirror at the back of the bar. A ghoul stared back at
her. The pale skin. Black shoulder length hair. Christ, Dani
thought, she looked transparent. She felt like a mouse that
had wandered into the lion's den by mistake. On the plus
side, she was still super young-looking for a woman in her

mid-thirties. That would count for something when she was up there on stage, right? They wouldn't know she was a sad, desperate soul on the brink of middle age, trying to claw back the years and restart her youth. Right?

In contrast to Dani's self-proclaimed frumpiness, Chiara looked like someone enjoying the first day of their summer vacation. She was dressed in a short blue dress with white polka dots. Her dyed blonde hair was loose and fell past her shoulders. Dani noticed that her sister's makeup was especially pronounced around the neck. More so than ever. Powder. Fake tan. Concealer. Chiara, it seemed, was working harder to hide the Burn.

Dani glanced back at the stage, checking on her pride and joy, a recently acquired Fender Flame Ashtop Stratocaster. The guitar was still parked in its stand, pushed up close beside the Marshall Amp.

"Can I get another beer?" she asked.

"Another beer?" Chiara said, staring at Dani's empty bottle. "Jesus, that'll be what? Your third or fourth in little more than an hour? Are you really that nervous Dani?"

Dani shook her head, not able to convince even herself with the gesture. "What's with all the questions? I'm fine. I just want a beer."

"Liar liar pants on fire," Chiara said, grinning from ear to ear. "Hey, I don't blame you for wanting to get wasted sis. Going up there on that big stage tonight all alone without a band. Just you, little Dani Pellerino from..."

"Dani Machete."

Chiara shot her hands up in the air. "Sorreeeeecy! I have to call you by your stage name now? Think you're a big shot now, huh?"

Dani laughed and pointed at a banner hanging off the wall at the rear of the stage. The words 'Dani Machete' had been painted in big, blood red letters on the front. It was a nice touch by Em, the owner, and one that had taken Dani by surprise as she'd walked into the Academy for the load in. It also made her a lot more nervous.

"Dani Machete," Chiara said, looking at the banner. "Cool name by the way."

Dani smiled. "Beats Dani McBride, that's for sure."

Chiara gave her sister a hard stare.

"McBride is *his* surname, not yours," she said. "That's a Mick surname. You're a Pellerino by birth."

"Whatever," Dani said, her elbows resting on the countertop. "Pellerino isn't much better than McBride. What's so great about Pellerino anyway? Tell you the truth Chiara, I'm not too enamored of our family name right now as it happens. Where are all the other Pellerinos tonight, huh? You think they're going to show up and offer a little support for what I'm trying to do here? I doubt it."

"C'mon sis," Chiara said. "You know Mom and Dad didn't take the breakup with Darryl well. They can't help it, they're old fashioned about things like marriage even when the marriage is a total disaster. The rest of the family aren't much better. They all think he was a fucking saint."

Dani reached over and brushed Chiara's hand away from her neck. "You're picking at it. Leave it alone."

"Yeah," Chiara said. "My neck's peeling a lot these days. I'll fix the makeup when we go upstairs."

Dani nodded. She didn't say anything else despite worrying about Chiara's Burn, which was a lot worse than her own. But at least Chiara could still hide the symptoms. Some people were so far gone that, no matter how many layers of makeup they put on, you could still see how bad it was. Those people usually stopped going out in the end.

Dani's Burn was mild in comparison to most, but she

went through the motions anyway, performing the same routine in the morning she'd been doing for months. First up, she'd put Aloe vera gel on to cool the skin, which was always hot in the mornings like it had been soaking in warm water overnight. Didn't help that New York was having a particularly brutal summer. If there wasn't any gel to cool the skin, and with all the panic buying that was a legit possibility, there was always plain yogurt or a cold washcloth to use as an alternative. That step was followed by a gentle cleanser and moisturizer treatment, and then a matte foundation with a cool bronzer to help the makeup blend in with the redness. All the information about effective skincare and a regular beauty regime to hide the symptoms of the Burn was available online. It was especially useful for the vast majority of men who'd never used makeup before.

Some people, like Raven, had fun with it. It was an excuse to go for extreme makeup styles, like painted skulls, werewolves, vampires, cat faces, and all sorts of other spooky things to turn heads in the street. It was Halloween every night of the week for those people.

Dani saw her sister's spidery fingers still chipping away at the loose skin on her neck.

"Pack it in Chiara."

Chiara's arm dropped to the side. She blinked as if someone was jamming a flashlight into her eyes. "What?"

"You're peeling again."

There was still a trace of white papery skin hanging off Chiara's neck.

"Was I?"

"Yup."

"Damn," she said, picking up her beer and taking a sip. "I don't even know I'm doing it half the time. It's like..."

"I know," Dani said, pushing her glasses up higher on her nose. "It's like someone else is doing it for you."

Chiara shoved the empty bottle beer away. "Christ, this is depressing. It's the same thing with Mel at home. Unless we stop each other, we're pulling big chunks of skin off at a time. It's gross and it's getting so bad that we've gotta watch each other twenty-four hours a day to make sure we don't unwrap ourselves and end up like those poor bastards in the cocoons."

She pulled on the sleeves of her dress, then slid off the barstool and went back to the fridge. Chiara grabbed two ice-cold Buds and walked back to the counter.

Dani pointed to the ceiling. "Is that wise? You heard what Larry said."

"Never mind what Larry said," Chiara said, decapitating both beers with the bottle opener and sliding one towards Dani. "We're celebrating. It's my little sister's first rock and roll gig and we're going to have a good night tonight no matter what. I for one, intend to get shitfaced and forget all about the world and its problems. You with me?"

Dani took the beer and clinked bottles with her sister.

"I'm with you," she said. "Guess I'd better get on up there for the soundcheck."

Chiara nodded. "Yeah. Before Larry throws a fit."

Dani slipped off the stool. She walked towards the stage and felt her legs shaking again.

"Nobody's going to show," she said, glancing back at Chiara. "Are they?"

"They'll show," Chiara said, walking behind her sister, scraping her shoes off the sticky floor. "People are desperate for live entertainment. They want to forget all this shit so you get up there and make them forget."

"But you haven't heard me sing in a long time," Dani

said. "What if it's just not there anymore Chiara? I can't be sure, you know? Holy shit, I'm thirty-five years old – what am I doing out here trying to be a singer? This is a mistake, this is such a big mistake."

Chiara clamped both hands on Dani's shoulders. "Stop looking for reasons to fail. Okay? I'm not going to let anything bad happen to you alright? Anyone who even hesitates to applaud after a song is getting their teeth punched out."

Dani felt a churning sensation in the pit of her stomach. She'd already puked once, about five minutes after arriving at the Academy.

She stared at the stage, hypnotized by its emptiness.

"You know they blame me for what happened with Darryl, right?"

"Who?" Chiara asked. "Mom and Dad?"

"Yeah."

"Forget Mom and Dad," Chiara said, leaning in and kissing Dani on the forehead. She wrapped an arm around her sister's shoulder and they faced the stage together. "They don't know what a slimy fucker he was. That's the thing with Darryl – he was always so good at putting on a perfect son-in-law mask at the right time. And then taking it off when it suited him. You know?"

Dani smiled. "He never fooled you though. Did he?"

"Not for one second," Chiara said. "I said this to Mel and I'll say it to you Dani. The day you walked out on that soul-sucking prick was one of the best days of my life. I even cracked open a bottle of Prosecco for God's sake."

"YO!" Larry called out from upstairs. "You ready to rock Dani?"

Dani was certain she'd collapse before getting to the stage. "Yeah."

"Sure she's ready," Chiara called up to the second floor, steering Dani by the arm and leading her towards the stage. "Just do your thing Dani. That's more than enough."

"You sticking around?" Dani asked.

Chiara shook her head. "I'm going to go up to the green room so I can start working through that crate of beer of yours young lady. Besides, the Loop's driving me crazy down here. Look at them – they're talking about the dust storms, as if anyone wants to hear about the fucking dust storms, blah-blah-blah. Good luck Dani, I'll see you up there when you're finished, right? Maybe that's where Em and Raven are hanging out too."

Dani looked at her sister. "You know there's a TV up there too. You can't escape the Loop that easily."

"Whatever," Chiara said, blowing her sister a kiss as she walked towards the stairs. "I'll drink myself blind and deaf if I have to. See you in a while kiddo."

"Don't touch anything in the green room!" Larry called out to Chiara. "All the TVs are connected"

Dani heard the sound of Chiara's laughter fading into the distance.

"Ready Dani?" Larry asked. "Let's start with the guitar and any effects you're using tonight."

"Yeah sure."

Dani climbed up onto the stage and walked over to the Fender. The guitar felt comforting as she fitted the strap over her head and pulled the instrument towards her.

This is really happening, she thought.

As she turned around to face the empty dancefloor, she could hear the TV behind her. Dust storms, Dani thought.

Was that really how it all began?

LOOP 2 - DUST STORMS

News Desk.

Twenty-four hours of non-stop premium news content, seven days a week.

Kurt Carpenter sits behind the desk while the blaring News Desk theme, a stampede of short angry notes, fades to a merciful silence.

KURT CARPENTER: Welcome back. So let's talk about these dust storms huh? No doubt you've seen the pictures by now or you've simply looked out the window and seen what's happening for yourself. It's quite incredible to say the least, not to mention a little alarming too. Let's see if we can't figure this thing out, right here on News Desk.

Carpenter glances at his guest. The camera cuts to a dark-haired woman in her fifties, slim, a tight-lipped smile on her face.

KURT CARPENTER: Dr. Karen Andrews is a leading international expert in climate matters and was previously Director of the University of Georgia's Atmospheric Sciences Program. Dr. Andrews, welcome to News Desk and first of all what's the latest update on these remarkable dust storms?

DR. ANDREWS: Right now Kurt, all I can say is that hazy skies and low visibility are due to continue for the next few days. The biggest update this week? Definitely that fast-moving shield of dust that swept westward through the Sahara before crossing the Atlantic and making its way into the Caribbean. That caught my eye for sure.

KURT CARPENTER: Yes, those familiar bright blue tropical skies of the Caribbean have turned into a weird brownish-gray color. But that's just one of many strange occurrences associated with the dust storms that we're encountering lately. Dr. Andrews, I guess the question I want to ask is, what on earth is going on?

DR. ANDREWS: It's an extraordinary situation. As you say Kurt, what's been happening in the Caribbean is just one of a series of major incidents this week. We've seen large plumes of dust sweeping the globe and almost all of it is clearly visible on the weather satellites. Even the astro-nauts on the International Space Station can see what's going on down here. High winds and choking dust have contributed to shocking scenes in the Americas, Europe, Asia, Africa, Australasia – they've all been affected. We've all seen the images on TV by now of famous global landmarks, the Statue of Liberty, Sydney Opera House, the Houses of Parliament, all of them cloaked in dust and caught under that dark orange sky. It doesn't seem real and yet here we are, looking at scenes reminiscent of the Dust Bowl days in the 1930s.

A set of images are broadcast over Dr. Andrew's words. Gigantic walls of dust smother city skylines. A helicopter flies over an endless highway jammed with cars. There are people standing on the road next to the cars, masks covering their noses and mouths as they wait for the traffic to start moving again. All around them, swirling brown fog chews up everything.

KURT CARPENTER: There's been a lot of speculation about these dust storms hasn't there? About the cause.

DR. ANDREWS: Yes, and due to the widespread nature of the storms, it's already been suggested that the cause is related to some activity in outer space such as a recent asteroid collision, which may have deposited the dust into Earth's atmosphere. It was excess dust from a previous asteroid collision, an asteroid that was allegedly ninety-three miles wide, that we believe led to the global cooling that triggered the Ice Age. But I don't think we need to worry about that Kurt. We're not heading for another Ice Age, at least not yet.

They exchange forced laughter.

KURT CARPENTER: Is that the most likely answer? That all this started in outer space?

DR. ANDREWS. Personally, I think it's the only answer Kurt. What people might not know is that there's always dust from outer space floating down to Earth. It happens a lot and in fact, the Earth gains approximately forty thousand tons of extraterrestrial material every year.

KURT CARPENTER: That's a lot of dust.

DR. ANDREWS: It sure is. That's about a thousand semi trucks' worth of interplanetary dust dropping down here every year. It's often caused by small pieces of asteroids or comets that come our way. But in fact, although that is indeed a lot, it's only a tiny fraction of the dust in our atmosphere. The majority of dust comes from Earth and it's made up of a combination of desert dust, volcanic ash and sea salt.

KURT CARPENTER: How worried should we be about this?

DR. ANDREWS: Let's not panic just yet Kurt. The dust storms will pass but having said that, there are definitely things we need to be aware of. Dust storms on this scale are a very big deal. They can affect climate, air, temperature and they can also influence ocean cooling. Dust is a carrier and it can transmit harmful pathogens to humans and it can also impair respiratory function. We're already seeing mass disruption in terms of transport and communications due to what's happened so far. And of course, there's air pollution to consider.

KURT CARPENTER: You mentioned pathogens Dr. Andrews. Correct me if I'm wrong, but I recall reading something this week saying that previous Saharan dust storms carried lethal meningitis spores throughout central Africa.

DR. ANDREWS: That's correct. There's strong evidence to suggest that dust can mobilize meningitis in the bloodstream. And not only meningitis, but influenza, SARS, valley fever – these can all be transported by dust too. Now here's something that maybe we should be a little worried about. Some of these storms we're seeing are the size of a major landmass so yes, if there's something to be carried, it's going to be carried far and wide and it's going to affect a lot of vulnerable people in the coming weeks. Most experts believe the worst of the dust storms will pass in a week or so. Maybe ten days. The intensity will start to wane and only then can we begin to assess the damage that's been caused. In the meantime, my advice is to stay indoors as much as you can and especially if you're at risk of developing health problems and complications. Turn on the air-conditioning and if you absolutely have to go outside, wear a mask to avoid breathing in the dust.

2

"Tell that asshole to fuck off right now!" Chiara screamed.

She was talking to Larry but looking at the uninvited guest standing at the green room door. "He sets foot in here and I'll cut his balls off – if I can find them that is."

She was pointing at Darryl McBride, Dani's estranged husband. Larry was the only thing standing in between Chiara and Darryl. He had one arm outstretched, trying to keep Chiara from coming forward, from charging at the man who'd knocked on the door just moments earlier.

Dani hadn't seen her older sister this mad in years. Chiara always had the fire in her of course, a cocktail of Irish and Italian blood that was guaranteed fireworks. She'd mellowed somewhat over the years and particularly as she'd approached the big four-zero, but was still a dormant volcano. Now, as she stood a few feet back from the door, Chiara's face was turning purple. Even more concerning, she was wielding Dani's machete in her right hand, stabbing the air with each angry syllable. This was the Dani Machete stage prop that just happened to be a real, double-edged cut-your-balls-off machete. It was legit. Anything less than the real deal would of course, have signaled the end of Dani's punk rock credentials before she'd even set foot on stage.

Dani was standing next to Raven, the bartender, and Em, who owned the Academy. They were gathered in the middle of the room, watching slack-jawed as Chiara's outburst intensified.

"Fucking scumbag," she roared. "How dare you? How dare you show up here today of all days?"

It had all been so pleasant five minutes ago. After finishing up the soundcheck, which had gone well apart from a bit of rogue feedback coming from the microphone, Dani and Larry had joined Chiara, Em and Raven, in the green room for beers, wine and downtime before they opened up the venue. Larry needed the break more than anyone. Poor guy was still sweating like a maniac, exhausted after one soundcheck. While the women had talked, he'd leaned his head back against the wall and closed his eyes. Told them he'd be alright after a quick nap.

Then, knock-knock.

At the sound of knuckles hitting the door, Larry had jumped to his feet like it was the FBI outside with a search warrant. He was still groggy as he opened the door, revealing Darryl standing in the corridor. Darryl was dressed in faded blue jeans and a Mets hoodie. There was a sheepish look on his face as he waved at Dani, who'd been chilling on the couch with her fifth, or was it sixth beer?

"Hi babe."

Chiara had exploded like a barrel of gunpowder. Now there she was, front and center, pointing the twenty-one-inch blade at a man who was still technically her brother-in-law.

"I dare you," she said, beckoning Darryl forward. "Come

in and see what happens motherfucker. See how far I'm prepared to go."

Larry thrust his arm out, trying to force Chiara backwards. "Calm down will ya?"

Darryl's meek expression didn't change as Chiara explained, in great detail, how she was going to carve out his eyeballs and play pool with them. For the most part, he ignored the elder Pellerino, concentrating his attention on Dani.

"Can we talk?" he asked. "Just a couple of minutes, that's all I'm asking here. We're still married after all."

He wasn't wearing any makeup. Nothing, not even a little concealer to hide the Burn which had left his face a hot, angry shade of red. His skin was flaky all over, with loose strips hanging off both cheeks and a little extra stuck to the chin.

"You've got a fucking nerve," Chiara said, inching closer to the door. "You ruined my sister's old life and now that she's finally trying to start a new one you think you can just show up here like a turd that won't flush? It's her first gig for fuck's sake! Does that mean nothing to you? Remember what music meant to her when she was a kid Darryl? Do you remember?"

"Relax," Darryl said. 'I'm not here to cause any trouble."

Chiara lunged forward, machete over her right shoulder. Both Larry and Darryl jumped back several inches across the floor.

"Trouble? I'll give you fucking trouble you piece of shit."

"Chiara!" Larry said, trying to shout but lacking the energy.

"Why don't you just keep peeling at that ugly face of yours until it comes off?" Chiara said, bringing the attack to a stop although she was still stabbing the machete in

Darryl's direction. "Just keep peeling all the way to Cocoonsville."

Dani glanced at Em and Raven and tried to smile. "I'll fix this," she whispered.

She walked past the pool table, running a hand over the tattered blue baize.

"Chiara. Chiara, stop it."

Chiara was still edging forward, the steel blade in her hand. Her casual, flat-heeled shoes scraped over the spotless carpet, one of the few things inside the lived-in Academy that looked new.

"Chiara," Em said. "I don't know what's going on here but whatever it is you guys better take it outside. That's if you still want Dani's gig to go ahead tonight."

"D'you hear that Chiara?" Dani said, stopping beside her sister and placing a gentle hand on her shoulder. Chiara's body was scalding hot. "It's okay."

"It's not okay," Chiara said, throwing Dani a furious look. "How can you say that? This guy took fifteen years of the prime of your life away. Trust me Dani, he's come here to ruin your big night and try to persuade you to go back to him and live the same half-fucking life that you've been living for years. Now I'm gonna do what I should have done when you were in high school and that's send this loser packing."

Darryl's voice was soft, almost boyish. The same tone he'd used in a million fruitless apologies. "I don't want any trouble."

By now, Larry was edging away from the door, unable to continue his role as peacemaker. "Is it hot in here? Or is it just me?"

"Stop peeling Larry," Raven said, an unlit cigarette squeezed in between her lips. "Larry! Cut it out man."

"LARRY!" Em yelled. "Did you hear what Raven said? Stop peeling."

Larry's hands dropped to his sides. He looked embarrassed, as if everyone had just walked in and caught him jacking off.

"I didn't even..."

Em walked over and took Larry by the arm. "Jesus, you're sweating through your shirt. C'mon, let's sit you down."

Larry let out a manic, frightened-sounding laugh as Em led him back to the couch. "Crazy," he said, taking the weight off his feet. "Who'd have thought six months ago that picking a little skin off your face meant..."

He shook his head and dug a hand into his pocket. Pulling out a fresh Kleenex, he dried off his face a little.

"You'll be alright Larry," Raven said, walking over to the fridge and pulling out a bottle of water. She handed it to Em who handed it to Larry.

"It'll cool you down," Raven said.

Larry took the bottle with a weak smile. "Hey Raven. Bet you're sorry you gave up smoking, right?"

The Marlboro Gold poking out of Raven's mouth twitched. "You better believe it."

"Chiara," Dani said, stepping in front of her sister. "Give me a minute with him."

Chiara shook her head. "Nope. You're not even getting a second."

"I'm not asking Chiara."

"You're crazy if you think I'm leaving you alone with that guy."

"We're not going anywhere," Dani said. "Listen, we're gonna stand right there in the doorway and talk for a minute. That's it. If anyone's earned the right to tell Darryl to fuck off it's me. Yeah?"

Chiara was still shaking her head but the fire had cooled a little. "Dani, look at the state of him. He's not right in the head. What if he tries something?"

Darryl stood in the doorway, hands clasped at the waist. Listening patiently.

"Just give me a minute," Dani said. "One tiny little minute. It'll be fine."

Chiara offered Dani the machete. "Want this?"

"No."

"Yeah well," Chiara said shrugging her shoulders, "just make sure you do tell him to fuck off. Because if you don't, the machete will."

The elder Pellerino sister glared at Darryl. She walked away, perching on the edge of the couch alongside Larry, Raven and Em.

Dani walked towards the door and felt a sudden twitch in her right arm. It wasn't too bad, so she ignored it.

She stood in front of her husband. "What do you want Darryl? Why did you come here?"

He smiled at her. "First of all, thanks for talking to me baby. I appreciate that. Look I know it's out of the blue me showing up here like this but I just want to say that I think it's great what you're doing here. I saw the banner downstairs. Man, that's so cool. It's going to be so cool tonight."

Dani's insides clenched at the smell of stale cigarette smoke. It was stuck to his clothes and skin. It was on his breath. "Yeah, it is."

"I've missed you. I've missed you so much Dani."

"Uh-huh."

"Saw your name on the poster outside. Everyone who

walks past the front door can see it. That's so cool man, really."

"Correct me if I'm wrong," Dani said. "But didn't you tell me once, no, many times actually, that music was a waste of time? Remember when I tried to get a band going after we got married? Get some recording time. Maybe cut a demo or something. Buying equipment was a waste of money, that's what you said. Same thing with investing time in writing songs. Everything was a waste unless it paid the bills. But now it's cool? The thing I love, it's cool now?"

Darryl looked at the floor. "I was wrong. You gotta understand baby, I was a giant, gaping asshole and I know that now. I was selfish and I didn't understand that there was room for those things in life too. But I can change like anyone else, can't I? Hell, I *have* changed. With everything that's going on, how can anyone stay the same? Makes you think about the big picture. You know? What you're doing here today, you're living the dream and that's a good thing. Hell yeah. It's what you should have been doing all along because life, well it's so damn short isn't it? I see now that you got used to being unhappy and I got used to you being unhappy, and that's my fault."

"What do you want Darryl?"

"I want you to believe me when I say that I've changed. I'll prove it to you Dani and I'll start by being there in the front row tonight. Cheering you on every step of the way."

Darryl was peeling. As he spoke, he pulled a strip of wet-looking skin off his right cheek and it came down like old wallpaper. Dani shoved his hand away from his face because that's just what people did for other people nowadays. Once upon a time they held doors open, but now they intervened if they saw someone, anyone, peeling their face off.

Darryl's blank stare fizzled out.

"Oh shit. Was I…?"

"Yep."

"It's getting stronger," he said. "Everyone keeps talking about the hatching and I used to think all that was bullshit, but now…"

"Why don't you wear makeup?" Dani asked.

"Too proud I guess," Darryl said, touching his face like it was a brand-new mask he was still getting used to. "Maybe I just don't see the point in trying to hide it anymore, you know what I mean? Maybe I don't want to line the pockets of a thousand startups, all of them trying to cash in on a global catastrophe."

He wiped the shine off his forehead.

"You're the love of my life Dani."

Dani shook her head. "I don't want to see you at the gig tonight Darryl. Don't be there, okay?"

Darryl smiled at her. He reached a hand into his pocket and pulled out his phone. He thumbed past the home screen and then flashed an image at Dani, showing her something with a scanning code on it.

"I've bought a ticket," he said. "Actually, I bought ten tickets because I reckon it's good to support upcoming creatives in their artistic endeavors. Everyone needs help at the beginning, right?"

"Well done Einstein," Chiara said, calling from inside the green room. "That's ten tickets that real paying customers can't get a hold of now. Ten more empty spaces in the crowd."

"I wouldn't worry about it," Darryl said, keeping his eyes on Dani. "Nothing fills up these days since most people stopped going out. But this way, you still get paid."

Dani began to close the door, forcing Darryl back out into the corridor.

"Go home Darryl."

"And don't come back!" Chiara yelled.

Darryl reached out and caught the door at the halfway point. "I can't be alone anymore," he said. "This thing, it'll take a hold of me if no one's there to stop me doing what you just stopped me from doing a minute ago. You understand babe? I don't want to become one of those cocoon things out there on the street with a name tag on my tank. I don't want to become one of those lifeless pods. I can't handle that Dani."

"Why don't give your mom a call?" Dani said. "I'm sure happy old Alice was delighted to hear I was out of your life, wasn't she?"

"I can't find her," Darryl said, his voice lowering. "I can't find Mom. I've tried the house, tried calling her friends, but no one knows where she is or what happened to her. It's like she just vanished off the face of the earth. For all I know, she's one of those cocoons already and maybe she turned when she was out for a walk somewhere. God knows. Oh Jesus Christ, why is this happening to us?"

"Bye Darryl," Dani said.

She forced the door until it clicked shut. But as she stood there, she didn't hear the sound of Darryl walking away.

"I'll be watching you tonight," he said, staring at Dani through the glass panels on the door. "Front row baby, front row."

LOOP 3 - THE BURN

Excerpt from an interview with WHO spokesperson and renowned dermatologist, Dr. Takeshi Watanabe. Dr. Watanabe is 49 years old and lives in Los Angeles.

The interview was conducted by Gerry McCready, a veteran journalist, originally from London.

NOTE: Two months after the interview, McCready was discovered in the cocoon state in his Hollywood home, alongside his wife Tracey. There was no sign of their nineteen-year-old daughter Emma.

GERRY MCCREADY: Dr. Watanabe, thank you for joining us today.

DR. WATANABE: No problem Gerry.

GERRY MCCREADY: Well, I think we can both agree that there's only one thing on everyone's mind right now. As a trusted news outlet, it's our duty to report the truth and the truth is that we've never seen anything like this before. We're talking, of course, about the condition that we're calling the Burn. There are Burn cases emerging all over the world, the numbers are rising dramatically and not surprisingly, panic is spreading. Now correct me if I'm wrong Dr. Watanabe, but the Burn isn't actually making people sick. And not everyone has it, because you're not showing any symptoms and neither am I. But when you step outside and look around, it's starting to seem like we're in the minority, right?

Dr. Watanabe nods.

DR. WATANABE: What can I say? There's a lot of information to unpack here Gerry. First of all, it's important for people to know where we currently stand with the situation. For anyone who hasn't been paying attention, the WHO has upgraded the severity of the Burn to pandemic and that's official.

GERRY MCCREADY: And if I may Dr. Watanabe, one of the strange things about the Burn is that it was never an epidemic, was it? What I mean is that this thing didn't start in one geographical location and spread from there. The Burn happened everywhere, an instantaneous global outbreak if you like. At least that's what it looks like.

DR. WATANABE: That's correct.

GERRY MCCREADY: We don't know for sure what caused this. As of now, citizens are advised to stay indoors although that's not mandatory because people need to go out for a variety of reasons. That may change as the government devises a strategy to beat this. The Burn, as far as we can tell, isn't contagious. Correct?

DR. WATANABE: We're pretty sure of that.

GERRY MCCREADY: Do you think it's airborne?

DR. WATANABE: I believe the recent dust storms are the most likely explanation.

GERRY MCCREADY: And yet there are many other theories popping up online. Some real whoppers too.

Dr. Watanabe smiles.

DR. WATANABE: Oh yes, I've seen them all. Some people believe the Burn is connected to the meteor that crashed in Russia last month in the Ural Mountains. Others point to nuclear leaks in Japan. We also have numerous conspiracy theories about cellphones. Wi-Fi, aliens and so on. But if you ask me Gerry, and although it's true we don't know for sure, I say the dust storms did it. That's the only credible explanation when it appeared in all four corners of the globe at once. We know that dust storms and sandstorm events are one of the most far-reaching vehicles for transporting potentially invasive microorganisms that are a concern for human health.

GERRY MCCREADY: Let's talk about the Burn itself. It looks a lot like sunburn doesn't it?

DR. WATANABE: The tests appear to confirm that. Regular sunburn occurs when UV rays from the sun reach the skin, damage it and cause mutations in the DNA. In that instance, it's the ultraviolet radiation that triggers the process but in this case it's something else and quite frankly, we're not sure what that is yet.

GERRY MCCREADY: What symptoms should people be on the lookout for?

DR. WATANABE: Dilation of the blood vessels, redness, swelling, inflammation – all of the common symptoms associated with regular sunburn. For all intents and purposes Gerry, this *is* sunburn, at least it is on the outside. The only abnormality here is the source of the damage.

GERRY MCCREADY: And what about what happens next? Will the damage heal like a regular sunburn?

Watanabe hesitates.

DR. WATANABE: We hope so. But with regular sunburn, some of the surviving cells may have mutations that escape repair and in time could become cancerous. We don't know if that's the case here and I wouldn't bother thinking that far ahead anyway because the answer won't reveal itself until much later. Right now Gerry, it's important for people to remain calm and to avoid aggravating any existing skin damage by staying out of the sun.

3

"I think it's going to happen tonight," Raven said. "Tomorrow at the latest."

Em stopped fidgeting with the label on her beer bottle. "What?"

"The hatching."

Em dug a swift but soft elbow into Raven's ribs. She jerked a thumb at Larry, who was sitting at the other side of them on the couch. His head was leaning back against the wall, sweat still pouring down his face. "Maybe it's not the best time to talk about that Raven."

Raven lowered her voice a little, but she kept talking. "C'mon boss, don't tell me you haven't noticed it. Feels like, I don't know, something's been different these past few days. There's this collective anxiety and it feels like it's swirling around, building up into something big. It's crazy I know, but I can't be the only one with this permanent sense of dread in my guts, can I?"

She wasn't. Dani knew exactly what Raven was talking about. It *was* a feeling, but that's all it was.

There were five people left in the green room after Dani

had closed the door on Darryl. They were split across two couches. Dani and Chiara were sitting on a ragged purple couch near the window, while Em, Raven and Larry were bunched up on an equally mangled red one. There was a small fridge near the red couch full of beers and snacks, and behind that, a four-panel door that led into a small bath and shower room.

Raven was still pretend-smoking the Marlboro Gold. Every now and then, she pulled out a chrome Zippo and thumbed the lid open, staring at the flint wheel with a look of longing.

"If you really want to quit," Em said, sounding like an exasperated parent, "why do you carry that lighter around in your pocket?"

So far, Dani had found Em to be a little stiff around the edges. It was kind of surprising for someone who ran one of the hippest live music joints in Manhattan. She was somewhere between forty and forty-five years old and as a black woman, the Burn was harder to see on Em than it was on those with pale complexions. With very little makeup, Em was still able to look like one of the Clean. She was long and lean, definitely pretty and yet Dani couldn't help but notice the resting bitch face that was Em's default expression. Dani tried to remind herself that the woman was having it tough. Her beloved business was in the shitter and that had to suck, especially after all the time and effort she'd invested in building up the Academy's stellar reputation.

"Throw the smokes away while you're at it," Em said, still looking at Raven like the bartender was a five-year-old on her way to the naughty step. "Jesus, quitting cigarettes ain't rocket science."

Raven groaned. "Aww man, who cares if I smoke or not?

The long-term impact of cigarette smoke on our lungs is the least of our concerns right now."

Nonetheless, she stuffed the lighter back into her pocket. The Marlboro remained wedged in between her lips.

Dani thought that Raven looked like a life-sized vampire doll. Her face was chalk-white, smothered in layers of makeup that was topped off with black lipstick and wild patterns of purple eyeshadow. She couldn't have been much more than twenty-two, and from the little Dani had picked up so far, Raven had studied psychology at NYU for a year prior to the Burn. The Academy was a part-time gig to help her through her studies, but now it was her only source of income.

Raven picked up a large bottle of Smirnoff off the table in front of the red couch. She poured a small glass and offered it to Larry, nudging him in the ribs to rouse him from the brink of sleep. Larry lifted his head off the wall, blinking hard. He took the vodka and emptied it at Raven's insistence.

Dani tried not to stare too hard at the sound engineer. They still had a gig to do after all and although she knew it was for selfish reasons, she willed Larry to perk up a little.

"Hey Larry," Em said. "You wanna borrow some makeup?"

Larry offered a weak smile in response. "Look that good, do I?"

"You look fine. But you're showing a little. I can help if you want?"

Larry dabbed at his brow with the Kleenex, shaking his head. "Let's talk about something else." He glanced over at the Pellerino sisters. "How are the tickets selling Dani?"

Dani felt like someone had reached inside her and tightened a knot.

"Uhh, I don't know."

"We got a few pre-sales," Em said. "But it's all about the walk-up tonight. Hopefully we'll reel in a few locals with a little spare change to spend at the bar."

Larry squirmed on the couch. "Jesus, I can't stop sweating. What's wrong with me?"

Chiara stood up, walked over to the fridge and pulled out a bottle of water. "Drink this," she said, unscrewing the lid and handing Larry the bottle. "Lay off the booze for a while, huh?"

Larry emptied the bottle in a single gulp. Then he groaned as if his thirst hadn't come close to being quenched.

"You feel something don't you Larry?" Raven said, inhaling the unlit cigarette and closing her eyes. "Like it's closer."

Larry nodded. "Yeah."

Dani was only half-listening to the conversations around her. She was thinking about Larry, thinking about Darryl and in particular, about the state both men were in. Nobody was going to say anything to Larry but it seemed obvious he was accelerating towards the end now. Fucking cocoons, Dani thought. That's all the world needs, more cocoons. They were everywhere, lined up on the sidewalk, on the road, in public buildings, public transport and in houses and homes all over the country. The authorities had long since given up trying to hide them because there were far too many to hide. Everybody knew. Everybody had seen them. Studies on the cocoons, what little had been done, were minimal and unsatisfactory. Most of the so-called experts were cocoons themselves nowadays so there were no ongoing studies to speak of. Who was supposed to remove them off the street anyway? The fake police had enough going on with all the looting and thieving every night. There weren't enough civilian volunteers and the military was a shambles. So the cocoons remained where they were, ornaments frozen in the exact spot they'd turned. Now they were just white shapeless lumps sealed inside glass tanks with identity tags stuck on the side. Nobody, not even the thieves or troublemakers, got too close to the tanks. Nobody wanted to see a reminder of what they were destined to become.

In New York alone, it was estimated that only a fifth of the human population remained. Everyone else was a cocoon.

Dani wiped the sweat off her face. It *was* strong tonight. The air was hotter and the ceiling and walls felt like they were closing in with a menacing slowness.

She finished her beer and grabbed a fresh one off the table.

"I believe in the hatching," Em said. "I do. And I've heard all the crazy theories out there about what's going to come out of the pods. But it's all bullshit. You wait and see; they'll come back to us as they were, a little dazed maybe but unharmed."

"Caterpillars and butterflies," Dani said. "One thing goes in, another thing comes out."

Em nodded. "They come out better."

'You really think people are just going to walk out the way they were?" Raven asked. "The way they were before?"

"Damn right I do."

"Now *that's* bullshit," Chiara said. "Face facts Em, the people inside those things are fucked with a capital 'F'. I know, I know, we're supposed to say nice things to them. We're supposed to talk to the cocoons, tell them we love them in the hope they can hear us like this is some kind of regular coma they're in. Bullshit. Some of those people have been like that for months now. They're going to come out, if they come out at all, either brain-damaged or dead."

Em shook her head. "Nope. They're..."

A high-pitched scream came from outside. It was a long scream that resembled the cry of a wild animal.

Then it was quiet inside the green room.

"What the fuck was that?" Raven said, standing up off the couch and staring wide-eyed at the window.

When no one answered, she crept past the purple couch and made her way towards the only window in the room. Pushing her face into the dirty glass, Raven looked out onto Bank Street and groaned.

"What is it?" Larry asked. He was perched on the edge of the couch like he was ready to start running. "What's going on?"

Raven's head made sudden bird-like movements as it jerked back and forth. "It's the cocoon across the street. The one opposite the front door."

"What about it?" Em asked.

"Not sure. There's a group of people standing around it."

Em stood up and dusted down her dark pants. "Yeah okay. But why the hell are they screaming?"

Chiara and Dani quickly joined Raven at the window. The Pellerinos stood on either side of the bartender and Dani strained her eyes for a good look at what was going on out there. It was getting dark outside and indeed, as Raven had said, a small crowd had gathered around a solitary cocoon tank located on the opposite sidewalk. Dani had noticed the cocoon, as well as others on the street, when they'd arrived but she'd paid little attention to them.

"Is that thing moving?" Dani asked, seizing the rims of her glasses as if somehow that was going to make them zoom in on the action.

There was another scream outside. It wasn't coming from Bank Street, but from somewhere else in the city.

Raven stepped back from the window.

"I used to hear screams like that all the time," she said, taking the cigarette out of her mouth at last. "When people first saw the cocoons, you remember that? Fun times, huh? They'd just appear suddenly on the street, in the back aisle of a store, in your garden or you'd walk into the kitchen one morning and your roommate was one of them. It all happened so fast. But in the early days of it, that's how people used to scream. Just like that."

Em joined the others at the window. She stared outside, her eyes cool and undisturbed.

"Maybe it *is* happening." She glanced left and right, trying to take in some of the other cocoons on Bank Street. "If it is, the show's off tonight guys. Don't think anyone's going to show up on the night of the hatching, do you?"

Em's words were a dagger slicing through Dani's heart.

"We paid to hire this place," Chiara said, glaring at Em. "Remember?"

Em pointed at the window. Excited voices were beginning to spill up from the street.

"You understand what's happening, don't you Chiara? Dani? If the pods are moving nobody's going to come to the show."

"So that one down there might be wriggling a bit," Chiara said, glancing briefly out the window again. "Big deal Em. That doesn't prove a damn thing."

"Even if it is the hatching," Dani said, opting for a calm tone in contrast to Chiara's volcano-on-the-brink-of-erupting voice, "it could take days for, *them*, to come back out. We've still got a few hours to go until showtime. People will get bored and they'll be looking for something else to do. And there'll be more of them on the streets after this, I reckon. They'll be looking for somewhere to gather."

Em sighed. "I don't know."

"I know you need the money," Chiara said, cutting to the chase as usual. "So let's get one thing straight Em – if you insist on pulling the plug for reasons that have nothing to do with us, we want it back. Every last cent and nobody gets paid."

Dani felt like throwing up again. Her comeback was hanging on a knife-edge.

"Alright," Em said after an obscenely long silence. "Have it your way. Just don't expect much of a crowd Dani because when word gets around…"

"Who knows?" Chiara said, sounding cheerful again. "If you're right about what's in the cocoons Em, people are getting their loved ones back soon and maybe they will be butterflies. This could be the best night ever. Maybe they'll walk out and their cancer will be gone. Maybe their aches and pains will be history. No heart disease. Maybe the paralyzed ones will be out of their chairs and breakdancing up and down the length of the city. Who knows? But if it's good then we got a celebration on our hands and what's a celebration without good music?"

Even Em had to laugh.

"Nice sell Chiara. Alright, but maybe we'll bring it forward an hour or two. If we can…"

"FUCK!"

It was Raven who killed the conversation. When the others looked at her, she was standing wide-eyed, pointing at the red couch.

"Larry's gone," she said.

LOOP 4 - CIVIL UNREST

From the UK:

'Disturbances have broken out across Britain today as patience with the government's initial lockdown rules wear thin. Many protesters claim staying indoors and wearing masks for essential outings does nothing to stop the spread of the Burn, recently declared a pandemic by the WHO. Many leading scientists have backed these claims, suggesting that the Burn is not passed between people but that it's airborne and caused by the dust storms that ran rampage across the entire world last month. Meanwhile, as food and money run low, people are calling for the lockdown to come to an end. The government is holding firm, at least for now.'

From South Africa:

'But of course, tensions are high here in Cape Town because no one knows how this thing is going to play out. We just don't know what happens next. This isn't something we've ever encountered before here in South Africa or anywhere else in the world for that matter. We don't know if it's going to go away by itself or how long it's going to be around. People are out here on the streets today not just because of financial concerns or to protest strict government measures. They're here because they're frightened and they want answers that no one can give them. The Burn is everywhere and it's clear that the numbers in South Africa are accelerating at as shocking rate.'

From Brazil (subtitled):

'Disturbing footage from Curitiba shows a father and son pleading with police officers for money on the street. The footage has gone viral, highlighting the devastating impact that the initial lockdown has had on many Brazilians. Several raids on grocery stores, as well as pharmacies for skincare products, have also been reported in Curitiba and in other areas of the country. In light of such disturbances, many are calling for the government to increase aid to those most in need. Many are also urging the Brazilian president to listen to the increasing number of scientists across the world who claim that lockdown and self-isolation are ineffective measures against the Burn.'

From Italy (subtitled):

'One line of business doing particularly well is the makeup industry. Skin creams too, are surging in popularity since the Burn. People are using a wide variety of creams and other products to both treat and conceal the redness on their skin. Supermarkets, stores and online suppliers report that they're struggling to keep up with demand and these shortages are leading to outbreaks of violence in some stores, with several arrests reported in Rome, Milan, Naples, and several other cities across the country.'

From New Zealand:

'Stores in Auckland, Wellington and elsewhere around the country are implementing a limitation policy on the number of skincare products that can be purchased by any one customer. The hope is that this will ease the widespread panic that's led to violent outbreaks inside many supermarkets and pharmacies.'

From the US:

'More and more people are returning to work this week as it becomes clear that the Burn is not contagious and as of now, is also not considered to be life-threatening. This mass return to work will encourage our flagging economy to get back on its feet, although the economy undoubtedly faces ongoing challenges in a time where one of the most frequently used phrases typed into Google is 'how do I stay safe while grocery shopping?' Perhaps a greater threat than the Burn itself is the continued threat of civil unrest, which doesn't seem to be going away despite the easing of the unpopular government restrictions. Shoppers continue to report genuine concerns about the fear of being assaulted as customers wrestle one another for access to beauty products on a daily basis. Besides this, criminal gangs are exploiting the situation and inciting violence in the form of looting and offering skincare products for higher prices on the black market. People might be going back to work in America but the social emergency is not over yet.'

4

"Didn't anyone see Larry get up and walk out of the room?" Em asked. She stared at the others with stern, schoolteacher eyes out of a Dickensian nightmare. Both her hands were on her head.

Dani *felt* those eyes. So much so that she was starting to feel like a little kid who'd just come back from a dog walk minus the dog.

"Weren't *you* watching him?" Em asked, staring at Raven.

"He was here a second ago," Raven said, her voice an octave higher than usual. "Look, he can't have gone far, can he? Maybe he just went downstairs for something."

"Downstairs for something. Like what?"

"I don't know."

Em stopped pacing the room and took a deep breath, in and out. Slowly. Her exhale sounded like a dying whistle.

"We're supposed to be looking out for him Raven. You've seen how far gone he is right? He needs us."

"What about you?" Chiara said, taking a step closer to Em.

"What about me?"

"You were the last of us to get up and come over to the window. Right? If anyone left Larry unsupervised on the couch, it was you. So quit hollering at Raven like it's her fault."

Em picked her beer, the bottle with the shredded label, up off the table. Without taking a drink, she slammed it back down again. "Shit. Didn't anyone hear anything?"

"Look we all got a little distracted back there," Chiara said, addressing the room. "But hey, Raven's right. Maybe he went downstairs for a little air or something. Maybe he just needed some alone time, not advisable but understandable if he's feeling like crap. He can't have gone far, which means we'll find him."

Em narrowed her eyes. "I hope you're right Chiara."

Dani didn't like this simmering tension between Em and Chiara. It was like they were trying to establish who was Larry's best and oldest friend, and therefore, who was in charge. Two alpha females jostling for supremacy.

Like a referee offering pre-fight instructions, Dani positioned herself in between the two combatants.

"Wherever he is he's not himself," she said. "So we'd better find him quick, just to be sure everything's alright."

Raven popped a fresh cigarette into her mouth and didn't light it. "Sounds like a plan."

But Dani found herself returning to the window again. Like there was a magnet pulling her over that way. The others went too, all four of them staring out across Bank Street and beyond. The small crowd across the street was growing. The cocoon was still inside the tank and everything seemed normal except that Dani thought she could see something running down the side of the glass. A whitish liquid. What the hell was it? Part of the outer shell? Whatever it was, it slid slowly down the walls of the tank, forming several small puddles on the inside.

"That thing's still moving," Chiara said.

"You sure?" Dani asked.

"You might be the better singer sis. But I'm the better seer. It's definitely squirming."

Dani watched, her face pressed up against the window. Chiara was right – something was happening over there, but they had to concentrate hard to see it as the light was fading. The women watched as small protrusions began to form on the white shapeless blob inside the tank. These lumpy spots pressed against the outer shell, swelling up like bubbles trying to free themselves from the host. The bubbles expanded so much it looked like they were all set to pop, before they shrank backwards and retreated once again into the cocoon. Then they'd come up, go back down, and this series of events would repeat itself all over again.

Chiara flattened her nose against the glass. "That's gross. That's like something out of *The Fly* for God's sake."

Dani hooked her fingers into the base of the window and pulled it up as far as it went. A gust of warm air blew into the green room. She leaned her head outside, taking in the numerous silhouettes gathered around the glass tanks, which were as common in New York City nowadays as yellow cabs had once been.

The sound of sirens was distant. So too was the blaring chorus of high-pitched security alarms.

Dani's arm twitched again. Felt like it was trying to jump free of her shoulder.

"You alright?" Chiara asked.

"Fine."

But Dani's rogue arm shuddered again. Then it jolted, like an eel freshly pulled out of water. The foreign presence inside was waking up, trying to get Dani's attention. And yes, it did feel more urgent than usual.

Fuck off you bitch, Dani thought. Not now.

"To hell with it," Raven said, staring at the tank across the street. "I need a smoke." She pulled the Zippo out of her back pocket again, thumbed the lid open and lit the Marlboro Gold in her mouth. Stepping away from the others, she inhaled and blew out a giant cloud of smoke that drifted up towards the ceiling.

"That's what I'm talking about."

"Shit," Em said. "We're getting distracted again by that thing. We need to go find Larry, like right now."

"Agreed," Chiara said, picking at the loose skin on her neck. The picking stopped before Dani could intervene. She could see the Burn slipping past Chiara's thick wall of makeup, especially around the neck. It didn't help that Chiara was fair-skinned either, taking after their Irish mother in contrast to Dani, whose olive complexion was courtesy of their old man and the Pellerino side.

"Before we go look for him," Em said, addressing the Pellerino sisters, "there's something I have to tell you guys. And it's not good news either."

Chiara leaned back against the pool table. "Great. Some bad news for a change."

"Yeah it's pretty bad. You might want to brace yourself as they say."

Em finished the last of her beer before continuing. "I probably should have told you guys earlier, but I didn't think it was that important."

"What is it?" Dani asked.

Em took a deep breath. "There are two cocoons inside the Academy."

Silence filled the green room. But it didn't last long.

"What?" Chiara said, looking at Em as if waiting for the punchline. "Are you fucking shitting me?"

"I ain't shitting you. It's the truth."

Dani felt like she'd been poked in the ribcage with a sharp stick. She looked back and forth between Raven and Em. "Two cocoons? In here?"

"It wouldn't have mattered," Raven said, smoking the Marlboro like it was a race. "On any other night it wouldn't have mattered a damn thing. It's not like we keep them in plain sight, standing at the front door and waiting to stamp everyone's wrist on the way in."

"Hell of a time to tell us," Chiara said, shaking her head. All things considered, Dani was surprised at how calm her sister was taking it.

Em was staring at the floor. "Yeah."

Dani took her glasses off and gave the lenses a quick wipe. She didn't want the others to see her on the brink of tears. Didn't want to see herself like that. There would be no gig, at least not tonight. As she stood there in that hot room, wiping manically at the lenses with her sleeve, it felt like she was sinking into the floor.

Who was she? Who was Dani Pellerino? Surely there was some kind of purpose to her existence, something beyond the inherent dissatisfaction she felt every day with everything. She'd hoped the gig might provide some answers. Give her a glimpse of something more.

Dani could hear the Loop on the TV, replaying the infamous Shadow Man clip. Chiara was right. Same old shit. What was the point of digging it up over and over again?

"So," Raven said, breaking the uncomfortable silence that lingered in the green room. "Now that everybody knows, how about we go find Larry?"

LOOP 5 - SHADOW MAN

He's a silhouette, cloaked in shadow.

There's not much else in the room with him. Only the vague outline of a closet at his back, as well as the figure of eight shape of an acoustic guitar propped up against the wall. Both objects are barely visible in the dim candlelight.

The speaker's voice is disguised by voice-altering software, rendering it high-pitched and mildly distorted. There's an eerie, electronic child-like quality to the voice.

SHADOW MAN: The truth hurts. Sorry but you're not going to hear it from the scientists or the politicians or the talking heads on TV. D'ya think I wanna do this? D'ya think I wanna come off as a crazy man, even to myself? To my wife? To my boy? Nobody believes me. Nobody. They don't *want* to believe me.

Pause.

Heavy breathing.

The Burn. It's even more serious than we first thought. But I'm sure a lot of you know that by now, eh? Even if you don't want to admit it to yourselves. For my part, I've always refused to use skin products and so maybe that's why I noticed the peeling early on and how bad it was getting. Yeah, have you seen it yet? Have you? My head looks like it went twelve rounds with a cheese grater and lost. Ha-ha! My arms, legs, chest, feet – fucking hell, it's all gone to shit. You should see me, but I don't think you're ready for that.

Shadow Man sways back and forth on the floor.

There's something else that you need to get ready for. It's a voice, a voice in your head. It's not your friend. Just to clarify, I'm not talking about the same inner voice you've known and trusted all your life, the one that's guided you through every decision you've ever made. This isn't *your* voice, it's something else. No, this isn't a regular sunburn. And that's what I'm here to tell you all. That's what I'm *trying* to tell you. The talking heads on TV, the suits and the medical people are trying to tell you that it's a one off caused by the dust storms and that soon enough, everything will be alright and it'll pass, that's what they say.

What does the voice in my head say?

Peel. Peel. Peel.

I don't want to. But sometimes it gets so hot and when you peel it feels like you're cooling down in the best possible way. It's like you're standing in a beautiful fountain on a hot summer's day with cool water falling down on your head and soaking your body. It's so good, it's one of the best feelings I've ever had. But when it comes, don't do it. Resist or you'll end up looking like me. You don't want that.

You know what the scary thing is? It's not the peeling and it's not the thought of death if that's where this thing is taking me. What I hate most of all is that I'm no longer in control of my body. There's been a mutiny, you know what I mean? I've got my own little Fletcher Christian inside my head, all hot and bothered, running around on deck and putting me in a little boat and setting me adrift. I've peeled so much, so deeply, that my wife has already thrown up twice just looking at me.

A woman's voice is heard off camera. Muffled. Shouting from a distance.

Shadow Man yells back.

Can I finish for God's sake? I didn't mention your name, did I? This isn't about becoming famous and it's not about money. You think I wanna do this woman? Somebody has to speak up first because this is going to happen to everyone and if they're not mentally prepared...

Pause.

Do you know what alien hand syndrome is? No, I didn't either but I know now. I bloody well know now. Here's a quote from a medical study that I wrote down for this video:

'Alien hand syndrome is a phenomenon in which one hand is not under control of the mind.' The study then goes on to describe it as 'observable involuntary motor activity along with the feeling that the limb is foreign or has a will of its own.' That's it, that's what's happening to me and if my hunch is right it'll happen to you too. Because the Burn is not the end of this, it's only the beginning.

It's time we faced up to what's happening here. Really faced up to it. To hell with the government and all the rest of 'em who're supposed to be in charge of us. They don't know what we've got. They're still talking about the economy for God's sake. Can you believe that?

5

The four women walked down the second-floor corridor, their footsteps a whisper on the hard floor.

Em was at the head of the procession while Raven walked a few paces behind, a cigarette wedged in between her black painted lips. Now that she'd started smoking again it was like she couldn't stop.

The Pellerino sisters were at the rear, following the two leaders closely.

They walked along the upper-level balcony which offered a birds-eye view of the stage down below. It was minimalist in terms of décor; mostly it was standing room only, a place that in days gone by extended crowd capacity during busier gigs. There was a tiny bar tucked into the far corner but with alcohol supplies at an all-time low in New York, it probably hadn't been used for months.

Dani looked above their heads. The recessed ceiling lights were weak, abandoning the foursome to walk in a swirling, murky gloom that wasn't great for visibility. Outside, the sun was in the midst of beating a hasty retreat behind the skyscrapers, leaving the city to an unknown fate.

"So where are they?" Chiara asked.

Em glanced briefly over her shoulder. "Huh? What was that?"

Chiara raised her voice a little. "The cocoons. Where are they?"

"Third floor," Em said, turning back to the front.

"Both of them?"

"Yeah."

That made Dani look up again. The third floor was directly above that black carpet of ceiling above her head. Although she'd visited the Academy twice before, once with Darryl to see a band he liked, and once with Chiara to discuss the details of the gig, she'd never visited the third floor. That wasn't open to the public as far as Dani knew.

"Dani!"

Chiara's head flashed in front of Dani, blocking her view of the immediate surroundings.

"Keep up sis. You're starting to fall behind."

"Was I?"

"Yeah, c'mon."

Dani nodded and the two sisters caught up with Em and Raven, who'd slowed down to wait for them.

"So who were they?" Chiara asked, as the group started walking again. "The two people upstairs. Who were they?"

Dani didn't want to know anything about the cocoons or more specifically, about the people inside them. She didn't want to know their names, who they were, what they looked like, what they did for a living, likes and dislikes – nothing. Niente. Why couldn't they just stay quiet until they found Larry and got him back to the green room? The answer to that was simple. Silence wasn't Chiara's way of dealing with stressful situations. Chiara's way was to talk and to keep talking and to ask questions, and she'd been like that ever since she was a little girl in the backseat of the car asking Mommy and Daddy why they were fighting when all the other kids in the Pellerino clan just kept quiet and stared out the window, buried their heads in a book, or put their headphones on to drown out the noise.

"The first one was a guy who came here to do a job," Em said. "An electrician. I don't even remember his name, what was it again? Mick, Mark, Marty, something like that. I didn't realize how far gone he was when he walked in that day. He seemed fine and Raven and Creed, my brother who was working in the office that day, both thought the same. He was working on the ceiling lights in the men's john up there on the third floor and well, that's where it happened."

"I saw him when he walked in," Raven said, blowing smoke out the side of her mouth. "That guy knew how to use makeup, so much so that he looked like one of the Clean for God's sake. He didn't seem sluggish either. Seemed alright to me. When he didn't come down after a couple of hours, I went up and found him, *it,* lying on the bathroom floor. Fresh and wet. Oh God, it was horrible."

"No wonder you can't give up the cigarettes," Chiara said. "Say, what the hell was he doing out working if he was so far gone?"

Dani glanced at her sister. "Money."

Em nodded. "Yup. People are good at hiding it, especially when they've got bills to pay."

"We called the number on the pamphlet," Raven said. "I thought we were going to get a bunch of government stiffs coming around, Men in Black style, breaking down the door as soon as I hung up the phone. All we got were a handful of fake cops, guys long past retirement age and who got exhausted just climbing up the stairs. They brought a glass tank, put it over the electrician and sealed it off with red tape. Told us to keep him there for now and hang a tag on the tape saying who he was."

"What did you write?" Chiara asked.

Em shrugged. "Electrician. It's all we could write."

"I hate walking past that bathroom," Raven said, stomping on the cigarette butt that she'd dropped on the floor. "There's this weird smell. That stinking cocoon smell, you know? Like rotten eggs and dog puke mixed together."

They reached the foot of a short, narrow staircase that led up into darkness.

"Here we are," Em said.

Dani looked up the stairs and felt her blood stop. "You really think Larry's up there?"

"Call it a hunch," Em replied. "It's dark and quiet on the third floor compared to everywhere else in the building."

Chiara looked at Dani, making a face that asked, 'did we really pay for this shit?'

Em took the first step, the wood groaning underneath her weight. Sounded to Dani like something big waking up below the floor. Raven switched on the flashlight on her iPhone as she followed Em onto the staircase. She pointed the white beam at the top of the stairs where it hit nothing but an empty wall.

"This is creepy as fuck," she whispered.

"Hey, what about the other one?" Chiara whispered as she and Dani stepped onto the stairs. "The other cocoon. Who was it? Mailman? Jehovah's Witness? Pizza delivery guy?"

Em stopped suddenly. Her shoulders labored up and down like it was hard to breathe.

"That's my brother. That's Creed."

The staircase stopped groaning as everyone came to a stop. Dani stared at the silhouetted backs of Em and Raven.

"Did they...?"

Raven turned around, her white face glowing in the dark. She reminded Dani of the girl from *The Ring*, the one that crawled out of TV sets and twisted the shit out of people.

"Same thing. The fake cops came, put a tank over Creed and stuck a label on the glass like he was baggage. They did that brief scanning thing, told us not to worry because they were certain that Creed was still alive and that when this thing blows over he'd be back to normal. Blah-blah-blah. Assholes, reciting a script in their heads. Couldn't get out fast enough. Right Em?"

Em nodded.

"As soon as Creed gets out, I'll call my mom in Arizona. I promised her that I'd call and tell her that Creed's alright."

Dani wondered if Em really believed that Creed was going to be alright. If so, and this really was the beginning of the hatching, then why wasn't she running to her brother now to welcome him back with open arms?

"My mom's stuck at home with my stepdad," Em said, still hesitating to cover those last few steps before the third floor. "He's been a cocoon for three weeks now but Creed's the only thing she talks about when I call. How is he? Any change? Did he move yet? Did they take any more scans? She's long overdue some good news."

Chiara edged past Raven, stopping beside Em near the top. "Okay, let me get this straight. The electrician's in the bathroom, right?"

Em nodded. "Right."

"And your brother? Where's he?"

"Office. Down the end of the hall."

"Okay," Chiara said, rubbing both hands together like she'd felt a sudden cold snap. "So we're thinking Larry's up here somewhere. Yeah? It's a bit cooler, it's dark and quiet. Alright, I say we do a quick sweep of the third floor and if possible, let's avoid the bathroom and office, okay? I don't think we're quite ready for that yet."

Dani stood at the back of the line, longing for another beer. She was far too sober for this shit.

They walked up to the third floor.

"Hey," Raven said. "Let me see if I can switch on the lights up here."

She put her hand on the wall, gliding it along the smooth surface until it landed on a silver toggle switch. Raven pulled the switch, triggering a brief seizure of light on the ceiling. The light stabilized although in the end, it wasn't much better than the dim ceiling lights back on the second floor.

The third floor was bland and unsettling. It was more like a traditional office building up there in contrast to the cool, grungy venue downstairs. The walls were dirty white and Dani thought she could smell something hideous coming up from the gray carpet at their feet. Or perhaps, she thought, remembering what Raven had said about the bathroom, the smell originated from elsewhere.

There were no windows and no pictures on the wall. It was a giant, blank space with an air of indifference. Nobody came up to a place like this because they liked it or wanted to. Only because they had to.

"Larry," Raven said, trying to both whisper and shout at the same time. "You up here man?"

The four women eyed one another, silently questioning their sanity. A moment later, there was another scream in the distance. This one sounded closer, maybe coming from Bank Street again.

"*Santo cielo*," Chiara said, her eyes widening. "Sounds like it's..."

A click.

The third floor was plunged into darkness.

"Shit!" one of them said.

Dani's heart was thumping. It was pitch black in the corridor and she couldn't see two inches in front of her face. In that moment, everything she'd ever been afraid of in her life was right there on the third floor, once inch away, reaching for her face and licking its lips in cold anticipation.

"You've got to be fucking kidding me," Raven said. There was a rustling noise. Seconds later, the iPhone flashlight was back on, the flimsy light parkouring off the walls and floor, confirming to Dani's relief that it was still just the four of them in the corridor.

"What happened to the lights Em?" Chiara asked.

"I don't know," Em said, looking down both ends of the corridor. There was more than a hint of concern in her eyes. "But if anyone else has a phone with a flashlight then I say get it out now. One isn't enough. Mine's back in the green room. As for the main lights, we can reset a circuit breaker from the inside but if it's something outside, I mean, if the whole grid's out we're screwed."

Chiara and Dani pulled out their iPhones and thumbed the flashlights on. Now there were three separate lights grouped together. It was a flimsy shield against the blackout, but it was better than nothing.

"My battery's on life support," Chiara said, bringing the cellphone to her face. "Dani?"

"Same. I got a charger back in the green room though. In my backpack."

Chiara sighed. "Okay. Let's just find that asshole Larry

before our phones die. This place is giving me the creeps and those screams outside aren't helping."

"We got flashlights in the office," Em said. "Proper ones."

There was a wry smile on Chiara's face. "Yeah and your brother's in there too. He can keep the good flashlights thank you very much."

"You afraid Chiara?" Em asked, turning her body towards the elder Pellerino sister.

Chiara nodded. "You'd have to be an idiot to be anything else right now."

"C'mon," Dani said. "Let's get a move on."

A sudden crashing noise made everyone jump out of their skins. Raven let slip a loud shriek that sounded like a startled cat. She dropped her phone on the floor, quickly bending down to pick it up again.

"What the hell was that?" she asked, straightening back up and pointing her light in all directions.

Em nodded towards the two doors on their right. The group had passed both doors just moments earlier. "It came from the bathroom. Gents, I'm guessing."

Dani hadn't even noticed the universal stick man and woman figures on the two doors. She looked at Em. "So that's where the electrician...?"

"Yep. That's it."

One of the doors was pushed open from the inside. A tall figure staggered through the vacant doorway, arms windmilling, legs like a toddler's first walk.

The shape came barreling across the corridor. Heading straight towards the women.

"Jesus Christ!" Chiara screamed. "What the fuck is it?"

Dani was the first to point her flashlight at the incoming shape. The light landed like a punch to the face, sending it swerving a few paces to the right. It was groaning. Sounded like it was trying to talk.

"Oh my God," Raven said, straining her eyes and trying to catch him with her own flashlight. "It's Larry. Look at the state of him."

It was Larry. His face was a mess of dead, hanging skin. His shirt had been ripped open and Dani could see more loose skin around the chest and in between the areas that he'd ravaged with his fingers, that terrible cocoon whiteness. It was flawless, like a pure gem buried underneath the skin.

"Get away from me," Larry cried out. His voice was muffled and Dani realized she couldn't see his mouth under all that loose skin. He was still peeling as he staggered back and forth, using one hand to unwrap the skin around his neck like it was a scarf.

"I'm so hot. So, so hot. Can't breathe…"

"Stop it Larry!"

Em hurried over, wrestling with Larry's rogue arm and trying to wrench it behind his back. "For Christ's sake, stop it!"

"Get away from me," was the dull response. "I can't stop it."

Larry pushed Em backwards and held his arms out, silently instructing the others to stay away. With the loose skin flapping behind him, he ran down the corridor, disappearing into the black hole that was the third floor.

"Larry!" Em cried out. "Come back you idiot."

"Move it," Chiara yelled, already running further into the darkness. "Before he disappears for good for Christ's sake."

The three torch bearers led the way, pointing their flashlights deep into the third floor.

LOOP 6 - RETRO VIKING

Danny Nilsson, aka Retro Viking, is a nineteen-year-old Swedish YouTuber with over a hundred million subscribers to his channel. He's the ninth highest-earner on YouTube, earning approximately $13 million dollars annually from a regular stream of content including video game news and reviews with occasional glimpses into his personal life. The latter uploads often feature his twenty-two-year-old fiancée Alexandra Koskinen, a Finnish bikini model.

This is Nilsson's final broadcast. It's an epic fourteen-hour livestream that's gone down in post-Burn legend.

His face is a red mess with long sheets of skin hanging from both cheeks, his neck and around the arms. Alexandra is sitting beside him at the Retro Viking desk. Her face is unmarked.

―――――

NILSSON: I look gross, I know I do. But it's really important that you don't look away. Okay guys?

Alexandra winces as Nilsson peels a long strip of dead skin from his neck. He leans closer to the microphone, allowing viewers to hear the wet tearing sound.

NILSSON: Don't forget to like, share and subscribe.

He laughs.

NILSSON: You remember Shadow Man, don't you? Do you remember the amount of hate that poor guy got after uploading his one and only video to YouTube? They said he was crazy and guess what? He wasn't crazy. And I want you to know Shadow Man, if you're still out there brother, that you're not alone. And anyone else who's as far gone as I am, you're not alone either. The authorities are still lying to us by the way, still telling us that this will go away in time and that everything's under control. But it won't go away. When will they admit that? I'm sorry my friends, but honesty is best from this moment on because he was right, this is no regular sunburn. Look at me, just look at me. Shadow Man didn't want to be seen but I think you need to see. So look at me.

Alexandra wipes her eyes dry.

ALEXANDRA: We must be honest. It's so hard, but we must be honest with ourselves and each other.

NILSSON: Now if you're one of my regular subs you'll know that I've been absent from duty lately. Haven't been posting much in the way of content.

Points at his face.

NILSSON: Now you know why. It sucks man, this thing, it really knocks you sideways, you know? I'm hot all day, sweating all night, and not getting much if any sleep at all anymore. Loss of appetite too, but that's not the worst of it. Shadow Man talked about the voice in his head and yeah maybe it sounded crazy at the time. But no, it's real. I can hear it; it's almost like my own voice but it's different. Keep peeling, keep peeling, it goes around and round my head like a mantra. And I do peel because I feel like I'm trapped inside an oven and unwrapping myself is the only thing that keeps me cool. That allows me to breathe.

Alexandra stares blankly into the camera.

NILSSON: Imagine being trapped under a pile of thick sheets on a hot summer's day. That's how I feel all the time.

Nilsson leans forward, sucking on a tricolored straw that pokes out of a vintage Pepsi cup. He keeps sucking until the familiar sound of the straw hoovering up air is unbearable. Then he falls back into his seat.

NILSSON: Ahhh, that's good. Anything cold is *soooooooo* good. Now another thing guys, I don't have much control over my right hand anymore and that's a real shame 'cos you know, that's my jerk off hand. But yeah, alien hand syndrome is real and it's something you have to be prepared for when this thing grabs a hold of you. I've lost count of the number of times I've woken up in the middle of the night, only to realize that my hand's been awake all along. Alexandra does her best to keep it off me, to make sure I don't hurt myself. But it's hard for her. And for me, it's too late. I know it is.

He peels, removing small but stubborn strips of skin hanging under his eyes.

The screen goes black.

A card reads:

'3 HOURS LATER.'

Nilsson's still at the desk, head buried deep in his hands. The top of his head, visible between the blistered fingers, is now hairless and as white as snow. He rocks back and forth to the sound of Alexandra weeping off-screen.

Nilsson lifts his head and faces the camera. The once handsome young Swede is now unrecognizable. Along with the absence of hair, his eyes are cloudy and unfocused. His skin is a glistening, newborn white and even now, as he pulls off his t-shirt to start work on the rest of his body, he points to the Like, Share and Subscribe icon at the bottom of the screen. The same icon he uses to close all his videos.

There are two hundred and ninety-eight million people watching.

6

"Let me guess," Chiara said. "Larry ran straight to the fucking office. Didn't he?"

It was Raven who answered. "Yup. That's where he's heading alright. It's locked but he's got a key in his pocket."

Chiara groaned. She looked back towards the stairs and then in the other direction, towards the office. "Looks like we're paying your brother a visit after all Em. Should've known this wasn't going to be easy."

Dani glanced at Em who didn't look too happy about the prospect of visiting the office.

"Let's get it over with," Chiara said.

They were halfway towards the office when they heard a barrage of footsteps in the corridor. This was accompanied by the sound of someone breathing heavy, like they'd just come back from a run. The noise was getting closer.

"Larry?" Em said, cupping both hands over her mouth to keep the volume down. "Larry, is that you? Get over here."

A human shape emerged from the darkness, running face first into a wide net of fast-moving iPhone flashlights.

There was a loud moaning noise as whoever it was, doubled over in exhaustion, hands clamped to their knees.

"Aww Jesus," Darryl said, sounding like he was on the brink of having a heart attack. "Get those lights outta my eyes will ya?"

Dani's knot tightened up. Just the sound of his voice was enough to make her insides clench.

"What the fuck are you doing here?" Chiara asked, looking at Darryl like he was a rat turd in her soup. "Can't you take a hint for God's sake?"

Darryl pointed to his chest, indicating he needed more time to get his breath back. "Something..." he said. "Something very...fucked up just ran past me a second ago."

"That was Larry," Raven said, her flashlight still mauling Darryl's face. "We're trying to get him back downstairs."

"Larry? The chink from the green room?"

"He's Korean," Chiara said.

Darryl rolled his eyes. "Like I give a fuck Chiara. Go join the PC police and start waving flags if it bothers you that much."

"You saw him?" Em said. "Didn't you try and stop him? Didn't you see how far gone he was for God's sake?"

"Stop him?" Darryl said, jerking a thumb over his shoulder. "That guy? He looks like something out of a goddamn horror movie, all skin and screaming his way down the corridor like the Mummy's Revenge. Touch him? For Christ's sake, get a grip."

Chiara spat out a vicious laugh. "You looked in a mirror lately Darryl?"

"Hey Chiara," Darryl said. "Why do you have to be such a ball-buster all the time? Is it because you're secretly in love with me or something? Jealous I chose your pretty little sister over you?"

"Yeah," Chiara said. "You're just so hot I can't help it."

Dani's voice was calm, in contrast to the others. "This isn't helping. What are you doing up here Darryl?"

"He was hiding," Chiara said. "That's what he was doing, right stud? Darryl McBride, high school superstar, the guy who jerks off to *Guns & Ammo* eight days a week. Up here hiding 'cos he crapped his pants when he realized the night we'd all been waiting for had finally arrived."

"Uhhh, has everyone forgotten about Larry?" Raven asked.

Darryl stared at Chiara as if she'd sprouted a third eye.

"Hiding? Are you for real? Hey Chiara, tell me something will ya? Did you dye your personality blonde too? Hiding my ass. I was up here looking for you guys, that's what I was doing. I was on Bank Street when those things started cracking open like chicken eggs. And it ain't just here. I'm getting texts from Joey in Cincinnati, Drew up in Anchorage, and Bobby in Denver. Shit's hit the fan ladies, just in case you didn't know."

"Thing is man," Chiara said, "you wouldn't have come up here to hide on the third floor. Not if you knew what was up here."

Darryl frowned. "Huh?"

Chiara held the iPhone flashlight up to her chin. She looked like someone telling spooky stories in the dark.

She spoke in a creepy whisper. "There are two cocoons. Here on the third floor."

"Bullshit."

"It's true," Em said, staring at Darryl. "Let me guess mister man. You were trying to hide in the office and found the door locked, right?"

"I wasn't fucking hiding," Darryl said, scratching at a small oasis of stubble on his chin. "What's wrong with you people? Why does everyone think I was hiding? And hey, if there are two cocoons up here, what the hell are you all doing running around like a pack of Buffy the vampire slayers looking for a chink that's beyond help? And what happened to the lights?"

Raven pointed her flashlight down the corridor. "We'd better get to the office."

"The office," Darryl said. "Why's everyone so high on getting to the office all of a sudden?"

"My brother's there," Em answered, her voice quiet and matter of fact. "And once we grab Larry and get him back to the green room, I'm coming back for Creed. I'm not leaving without my brother."

Raven's jaw dropped. "What? You can't be serious Em, we don't know what we're dealing with yet. We don't know what's coming out of those cocoons."

"He's my brother."

"You've already said that like a million times already," Chiara said. "We get it."

"What if it was Dani?" Em said, turning to Chiara. "Would you just leave her, not knowing if she needed you?"

Chiara didn't answer.

"Oh Jesus, Mary and Joseph Christ," Darryl said, his voice like a foghorn inside a phone booth. "You're one of those geniuses who think people are just going to walk out of the cocoons the same as they were before, just like nothing happened. Yeah right."

Em's upper lip curled into a snarl. "You an expert or something?"

"Newsflash sweetheart, I'm a realist. Your brother ain't your brother no more. Comprende? Best thing you can hope for is brain damage but death's still the favorite with the bookies. And your chink friend is a goner too so let's start using our heads and get the hell out of here."

Raven pointed the flashlight at Darryl's eyes, making him squint and turn his head away.

"Knock it off!"

"I don't know who the hell you are man," Raven said. "But let me tell you something. We're not leaving Larry alone up here."

"We're wasting time," Dani said, the first one to start walking again.

The others followed. Even Darryl went with them, although he continued to grumble at the back of the line.

It was a short walk to the office. They came to a stop in front of a large oak panel door with a faded 'Staff Only' sign on the front in printed red letters. The door looked like it had been there for decades. There was no glass on the outside like there was with the green room door, which meant no way to peer inside and take stock of the situation. To do that, they'd have to go in.

Em squeezed past the Pellerino sisters. She demonstrated all the enthusiasm of someone about to walk the plank.

She stopped in front of the door, staring at the handle as if hypnotized.

"I..."

"Em," Raven said, stepping up alongside her boss. "Give me the key. I'll do it."

Em shook her head. "Nah, I'm fine."

She held the key, a silver Yale, in between forefinger and thumb. Dani wondered how many times she'd used that key already. How often had Em come here in the small hours, creeping away from the rest of the world, to visit her baby brother, talking to him and hoping that her voice would keep him close? There were people all over the world who sat with their loved ones' cocoons for hours, talking, reading stories, playing their favorite music and podcasts on loop. They swore it would pay off in the end.

Em slid the key into the door. The noise of such a simple act was incredible.

Dani glanced over her shoulder and saw Darryl standing apart from the others, shaking his head and mouthing the word 'stupid' over and over again.

Em leaned her shoulder up against the door. She was about to say something when they heard a series of repetitive thumps from inside the office. Sounded like stamping feet. The stamping was followed by a tinny screech, then a long scraping noise that might have indicated something being dragged across the floor.

"Let's get out of here," Darryl said. "This is the stupidest thing I've ever seen."

Em stared at the door, a haunted look on her face. "He needs my help."

She turned the key in the lock and gently pulled down the handle. "Creed."

"Are you bitches fucking crazy?" Darryl hissed, backing off further down the dark corridor. "The chink is dead, your brother's dead. You can't save dead men."

No one answered and Darryl continued to hiss and mumble in the background. Fucking this, fucking that.

Em pressed her body against the door again. It groaned open. They stepped inside, into a mere trickle of distant, orange streetlight that filtered in through a half-moon window at the back. The impact was minimal. Everything in the room was cloaked in shadow.

"Creed?"

Dani's nostrils twitched. The scent that lingered in the air was sweet and sickening.

They pointed their flashlights around the room, the light doing a jittery dance off the office walls. There wasn't much to see. A tall closet at the back, a desk, two computer swivel chairs and a desktop tucked into the left-hand wall – that was it when it came to the furniture.

One of the flashlights landed on something on the floor. It was the government-issued glass tank with the label attached. It was lying on its side on the floor.

"Oh shit," Raven whispered as all the flashlights met in the center of the room.

The cocoon had burst, that much was clear. There were chunks of casing everywhere, discarded spongy pieces lying alongside glass fragments from a giant hole in the shattered tank.

One of the flashlights skipped to the right, lowering onto the carpet, where something was moving.

"Larry?" Raven said. "Is that you?"

Em shoved her way past the others, grabbing Raven's flashlight and tracking the movement on the floor. She made a loud gagging noise.

Dani's blood was like ice water in her veins. That awful stink, sweet and deadly, was getting stronger. There was a lip-smacking sound that was all wrong.

She tried to focus, to see what Em had seen.

The shape on the floor was big. As the iPhone light flooded its back, it turned its head around slowly. That was when Dani saw something else on the floor. Something lying beside the big shape.

It was Larry. What was left of him.

"Oh Jesus," Dani said.

Em staggered backwards, hand clamped over her

mouth. She screamed, a muffled cry of terror. "Creed. Oh my God, Creed is that you?"

The big shape rose to its feet. It turned its body towards the women, still bathing in the iPhone light beams.

Em reached for the shape but Chiara instinctively grabbed a hold of the outstretched arm.

"Don't even think about it."

Em was spilling over with emotion. Her eyes watered. Her lips trembled.

"He's my brother."

Chiara maintained a solid grip on the bigger woman's forearm. Then, like a parent leading a hungry kid out of a candy shop, she forced Em towards the door.

"C'mon, we're going. Everyone."

"Creed!" Em cried out. "It's Em, your sister. I've come to get you."

Creed began to approach the four women at the door. He was naked from head to toe and as he came closer, Dani noticed that his eyes had rolled back in their sockets, leaving only the whites visible. His skin, which Dani assumed had been the same dark brown color as Em's before the cocoon, had faded like a pair of old jeans. Now it was almost transparent.

"Look at his hands," Raven whispered.

More specifically, it was the knuckles that caught the eye. They were tall and sharp, like a series of mini-daggers sprouting out of Creed's hands. There were tiny fragments of glass stuck to the knuckles, as well as a lot of blood, most likely coming from Larry.

In that moment, Dani realized that the glass tanks designed to contain the hatchlings would be of no use whatsoever. With dagger-like knuckles, they could just smash their way to freedom whenever they wanted.

"Oh shit," she whispered. "This is bad."

The worst thing was the grin on Creed's face. It was a gargoyle-like grin that pushed the facial muscles to extremes. It was a dead-eyed, impossible smile that, combined with the white eyes and dagger knuckles, made for a truly horrific sight coming across the office towards the women.

The hatchling's jaw went up and down. It was stiff like a ventriloquist's puppet that hadn't been used in years.

"*lurvyoorr, lurvyoorr.*"

The voice was thin and raspy.

"That's not Creed," Raven said. "I don't know what that is but it isn't Creed."

"It *is* Creed," Em said, digging her heels into the floor and refusing to back out the doorway with Chiara.

Dani couldn't take her eyes off the hatchling. Off the grinner. It was the sameness and yet the otherness of it that was so unsettling. They *were* the people they'd once been and yet it was obvious that they weren't. Differences were both minimal and profound.

It didn't look good for the optimists. For those who'd believed in a happy ending.

The grinner turned its head away from the marauding flashlights. Retreating back into the office, it dropped to its knees and rediscovered Larry's mangled corpse. It reached towards the massive hole in the dead sound engineer's chest, the hand sliding in and out in a slow, careful rhythm. Each time it pulled the hand out, the grinner licked its fingers dry before going back in.

"We need to get out of here," Dani said. "Now. Quietly, quickly."

As if it had heard her, the grinner jumped back to its feet. It stared at the small group, still huddled together in the narrow doorway. Creed's colorless eyes narrowed, the jaw still going up and down like a robot.

"*muneeeeee, allyooorwawwnt.*"

"What the fuck is it saying?" Chiara asked. She still had Em's forearm locked in a tight grip. "Does anyone know what it's saying?"

"Creed," Em said, pleading with her wide eyes and outstretched hands. 'Do you remember me Creed? Em, it's Em! Your sister."

The grinner blinked, turning its head in the direction of Em's voice.

It hurried across the room with short scurrying steps. Reaching both arms towards them, all ten snake-like fingers twitching in midair.

Chiara yanked on Em's arm and she managed to pull the Academy's owner through the doorway. Dani and Raven were right behind them.

The grinner chased after them. With her back to the door, Dani heard a loud squelching noise as Creed trampled over pieces of Larry and the wet cocoon that littered the floor. When she turned around, Dani saw it coming, the long, loose limbs flapping ape-like as it hurried towards the doorway.

"The door!" Dani yelled.

Raven was on it. She slammed the door shut just in time and there was a loud thump as the grinner's body slammed against the wood.

"*allllyoooorwawwnt!*"

Raven struggled with the Yale in the lock. After fumbling around, she turned it and pulled the key out. Her face was as white as it had ever been.

"Let's get the fuck out of here."

They ran back downstairs to the second floor, pointing

their feeble light in front of them. Darryl was already halfway down the mid-level corridor, approaching the first of the two staircases that descended to the first floor and the front door.

"Move!" he called back to the others. "Before that thing breaks down the door and catches up with us."

Dani could still hear the grinner banging on the door upstairs. Sounded like a giant banging its fist against the roof. One that was enraged, perhaps even frightened of being left alone.

There was a clicking noise above their heads as they ran full throttle towards the stairs. The ceiling lights flickered and after a long, hanging pause, the lights came back on much to the relief of everyone. All the micro-details of the Academy's interior returned. Dani saw A4 posters advertising gigs, promos for drinks promotions and upcoming club night flyers all stamped to the wall. Dirty floors, a mop bucket, and a plastic cup of water sitting on the ledge. Everything was welcome, but none more so than the light itself.

"Thank God," Chiara said, lowering her iPhone to her side. "Let's get out of here."

They ran to the stairs and stopped.

Darryl was standing at the top of the upper staircase, staring down at the first floor. He was shaking his head.

"What are you doing?" Dani asked. "Keep moving."

Darryl pressed a finger to his lips, then pointed downstairs. His arm, which Dani noticed was trembling, shifted a few inches to the right, towards the bar.

"What is it Darryl?"

Dani crept towards the top of the stairs, recognizing an unspoken call for silence from her husband. She leaned over the railing. Chiara, Raven and Em did likewise.

"Fuck," Raven whispered. "You gotta be kidding me."

The electrician was patrolling around the bar. He was stark naked like Creed, his skin a ghoulish shade of pale that matched the emptiness of his colorless eyes. At that moment, he was on the countertop, doubled over, his nose pressed up tight against the filthy wood and inhaling what could only be the scent of stale alcohol.

There was a loud groan. It was impossible to tell if it was an expression of disgust or pleasure.

"Son of a bitch," Chiara whispered as she retreated behind the railing. "Now what do we do?"

LOOP 7 - THE DEBATE

Robert Nesbit, renowned political commentator and presenter of popular quiz show BrainGame, is hosting a televised debate.

The title:

'LGO vs. Q: Who's Right?'

The setting is a traditional community hall with a low stage, wooden floor, and tall ceilings with elegant lantern lights. Participants on both sides of the discussion are seated in three rows of wooden benches on the main floor, the two teams facing opposite one another.

Nesbit stands in the center of the hall, microphone in hand.

The LGOs (Life Goes On) representatives are on Nesbit's right. The Qs (Quarantiners) are on his left. Both sides have a designated spokesperson.

———

ROBERT NESBIT: Let's talk about the Nilsson effect, shall we? As we all know, one of the world's most popular YouTubers, Danny Nilsson, aka Retro Viking, inspired a disturbing trend of young people filming themselves entering the cocoon state. While many criticize the now cocooned influencer for his irresponsible actions, others have defended him saying that he was only doing what he'd always done on his channel, which was to create relevant content for his fans. Let me ask you Jenny – what do the LGOs have to say about it? Nilsson was indeed carrying on as normal which aligns with LGO philosophy, does it not?

Jenny McDermott, thirty-seven-year-old LGO spokesperson, stands up to address the room.

JENNY MCDERMOTT: LGOs believe that life goes on despite the Burn, but that doesn't mean we support stupidity. By all means, if you've got a YouTube channel and it's keeping you busy or better still, providing you with an income during hard times, keep making your videos. Do your thing, spread encouragement and positivity throughout the online community. But to peel yourself into a cocoon just to secure your biggest audience and make thousands of dollars that you can't even collect – that's stupidity. No one here is promoting stupidity, so no, Danny Nilsson is not aligned with LGO values.

ROBERT NESBIT: Well he might collect the money yet Jenny. After all, we don't know what happens next, do we? And that's a big payday waiting for Danny if he comes through this period of ummm, involuntary downtime, unscathed.

JENNY MCDERMOTT: Life Goes On, at its essence, is about hope. We advocate for a healthy work and life balance during the crisis wherever possible. Because if we do get through this Robert, we can't allow the economy to crumble. That would be a disaster for all of us to wake up to on the other side. Therefore we advocate getting into a routine of work, exercise and yes, keep bars and clubs open. Let's do normal things. Let's be normal. Go to the movies, go to a gig, and visit your friends. Be normal. We know the Burn isn't infectious so spend money whenever you can to ensure a thriving economy survives the pandemic. The Qs want everyone to hide away in their homes and let everything crumble to dust. That sort of defeatist behavior will be the end of us, not the Burn.

ROBERT NESBIT: Malik, from a Quarantiner perspective, what do you think of the Nilsson effect?

Malik Jafari stands. Jafari is a fifty-eight-year-old man with only a hint of the accent he brought over from his native Palestine thirty years ago.

MALIK JAFARI: Thank you Robert. Danny Nilsson and all the other YouTubers cashing in on this crisis are simply doing what they've always done. Life goes on indeed, especially if you're starved for attention like these poor children must have been all their lives. They, like so many other LGOs, are not taking this crisis seriously and instead, they see it as an opportunity to create unique content and gain recognition for their brands. They don't really care about the root issues. They don't care about anyone but themselves. Isn't that so Miss McDermott?

ROBERT NESBIT: Hang on Malik. Do you really believe that people aren't taking this crisis seriously? That's a big statement to make.

MALIK JAFARI: Robert, only the Qs are taking this seriously. Is it too much to ask people to stay at home and only to venture outside when absolutely necessary? Jenny says this isn't infectious but...

Jenny is back on her feet.

JENNY MCDERMOTT: It's not infectious. The Burn is *not* infectious. That's been proven beyond doubt by science!

MALIK JAFARI: Nothing is beyond doubt. How can you speak with such certainty when so little is known about this plague that haunts us? How can you say life goes on, go to the movies and meet other people, as if mental instability wasn't at an all-time high? What do we know about this thing? What do we really know?

JENNY MCDERMOTT: We know a lot of things Mr. Jafari. We know the dust storms...

MALIK JAFARI: No! There's no evidence to suggest it was the dust storms. That remains pure speculation on our part. Where is the evidence?

JENNY MCDERMOTT: Oh for crying out loud. What else could it be? Something is growing in our bodies, soaking up nutrients and changing us from the inside out, and it was carried here by the dust storms. How else could it have traveled so far and so fast? And another thing we know Mr. Jafari, is that people are still alive in the cocoon state. We know this from the scans. Why then is it so impossible for you to believe that these people won't come back, and that a full recovery is on the cards, both personally and collectively?

MALIK JAFARI (*shakes head*): What else in nature goes into a cocoon and comes out the same? We must stay in quarantine until these *things* reveal themselves.

JENNY MCDERMOTT: Things? They're people for God's sake and what's more they're *our* people. We can't just give up on them. We've also got the Clean out there, millions of people all over the world who didn't get the Burn or those fortunate enough to lose their initial symptoms within a few days. Scientists are studying these people as we speak, trying to discern if there's some specific habit or behavior that immunized or healed these people. There's a lot to be hopeful about Mr. Jafari.

MALIK JAFARI: The Clean account for a miniscule fraction of the global population. Less than one percent.

JENNY MCDERMOTT: But they're still out there. My point is that there's a way out of this thing and that hiding in our houses and apartments short term is going to do irreparable harm to the American economy.

McDermott's last statement is rewarded with a round of applause from her LGO colleagues sitting behind her.

MALIK JAFARI: *(shouting over the applause)* You're crazy! You're crazy! Talking about money when we have these things growing inside us right now. Have you forgotten? Who amongst you LGOs has ever seen anything like this in your lifetime? There's a virus growing inside us and it's perfectly designed to attach to the host, a perfect little invasion that turns our bodies and minds against us. Our science is helpless. Science cannot even *see* it. There's only this sunburn and then one day, your inner thoughts are muddy and soon you realize that they're not your thoughts anymore. This thing is talking to you. We're being taken over by something we cannot comprehend and you want to stand in front of me and talk about the economy?

The Qs applaud.

Jafari holds a hand up, requesting immediate silence.

MALIK JAFARI: Isn't it better to be safe? Isn't it better to stay with your family, to share information online and to dedicate yourself to a regime of inner resistance against the voice in your head? The government doesn't have a clue what to do about this. We haven't heard from the President in over a week now. Where is our leader? Where is he? No, we must lead ourselves from now on.

Applause.

The host gestures for McDermott to respond.

JENNY MCDERMOTT: You talk about inner resistance Mr. Jafari, but we can't expect people to beat this thing on their own. Isolation is dangerous right now. Very dangerous.

MALIK JAFARI: Quarantine is not perfect, but it's better than the LGO philosophy of pretending like nothing is happening.

JENNY MCDERMOTT: Nobody's saying the Burn isn't happening. Who said that? But turning tail, hiding and hoping for the best isn't a solution. The cocoons have done us no harm and what's more Mr. Jafari, the people in those tanks are our sons, daughters, fathers, mothers, grandparents, friends, neighbors and so on. Do you want us to turn our back on them? They need us more than ever. Let's be there for our people and ensure that the world is still intact when they return to us. Their jobs, their security – let's take care of these things in their absence. They *will* come back one of these days. And the first thing they'll do? They'll thank us for keeping the house in order.

Debate clip ends.

7

Em locked the green room door and peered through the twin glass panels.

"He hasn't followed us. I think we're okay."

"Holy shit," Darryl said, pacing the room, constantly touching the side of his face where a pocket of blistery skin bubbles was coming up. "We're trapped. We're fucking trapped in here with two of those things."

Chiara nodded. "Thanks Captain Obvious. Anyone got any ideas?"

"I've got one," Raven said, lighting up a fresh Marlboro Gold. "I'm going to smoke myself to death right here in this room. I'm serious. I'd rather die of cancer than get my heart ripped out like that. Did you guys see what Creed did to Larry? Did you see what he did?"

Muttering something to herself, she hurried over to the fridge and grabbed a Bud from an unopened six-pack on the top shelf. Ripping the pull-tab backwards, she gulped the beer down. It was gone in less than a minute.

"Damn good."

Taking out the now five-pack, Raven held it aloft, clutching the plastic ring binding like a strap.

"Anyone else looking for a one-way ticket to oblivion?"

"Hell yeah," Chiara said, taking two Buds off Raven and offering one to Dani. Dani opened the can and took a sip but the beer didn't taste as good as it had earlier. It was warm, despite having been in the fridge for almost an hour. There was no flavor to it either. It was a bland, tame liquid.

"I'll take one of those bad boys," Darryl said, holding a hand out like he was ready to catch the ball. "Pass it over here will you?"

Chiara made a tut-tutting noise. "It's Dani's rider. If you want a beer Darryl, you have to ask your soon to be ex-wife. Nicely if you please."

"Huh?"

"For Christ's sake just take one," Dani said, pointing Darryl towards the fridge. She wasn't in the mood to listen to another skirmish between her sister and husband.

Darryl opened a can and drank like the survivor of a shipwreck who'd just found fresh water.

"Holy Mary mother of God," he said, tossing the empty can back onto the table. He belched and laughed like it was the funniest thing ever.

"You wanna drink Em?" Raven asked, looking warily over at her boss. "Anything?"

Em was standing apart from the others, leaning her tall frame up against the pool table. "Why was he grinning like that?" she asked, aiming the question at no one in particular. "I think when he saw me, he was trying to tell me something. But what? What was he trying to tell me?"

No one dared to come up with an answer. Instead of talking, they drank. As Dani worked her way through a disappointing beer, she glanced at the TV on the wall. The

Loop, still the fucking Loop, on and on it went like infinity. Chiara was right about one thing. If the Loop ever went down, they'd know for sure that the last strand of civilization was no more. Because if people weren't selling and buying advertising space in between the Loop's endless reruns then humanity was surely dead.

Dani stared at the screen. They were replaying clips about the president and how he'd turned from the CEO of Planet Earth into a white blob in a tank. There were images of the front lawn outside the White House, spilling over with Apache helicopters, jeeps and trucks by the dozen. There were people dressed in camouflage, running back and forth across the lawn, all yelling stuff to one another, looking all serious and grim and shit.

Dani felt like she could recite the reporter's words off by heart:

'Looking back now, we must remember that the president was skeptical of initial reports of the Burn, calling them 'hocus pocus'. It's also been widely reported that as the cocoons became an undeniable fact, the president wanted them rounded up, taken off the streets and out of homes, and hidden away under secure lock and key.

Well, that didn't happen. And what's become clear today Kurt, is that the Burn has no respect for social status, fame or riches. It doesn't matter if you're a king or a queen or if you're the winner of the Nobel Peace Prize. And it doesn't matter if you're the President of the United States because, and I'm sorry to have to confirm this to our viewers, but the rumors are true. The president is a cocoon. A White House insider tells us that his condition deteriorated last night and that he was locked in the Oval Office with guards until the transformation was over. No footage of the presidential cocoon is available.'

Dani walked over to the window. Bank Street was empty,

but she could see the remains of the cocoon across the street and the empty tank, which had been tipped onto its side and left to roll off the sidewalk and onto the road. Fluorescent puddles, small dots of color, left a trail that led away from the tank like tiny footprints. Glass fragments littered the road, making it look as if it had rained diamonds down on New York.

"Well, now we know."

"Know what?" Chiara asked. "What do we know?"

"We know what's in the cocoons," Dani said, turning around to face the room. "We know they're not friendly. Far from it."

"Do we though?" Raven asked. She was perched on the beer table, working on her resolution to smoke herself into an early grave. Already the room reeked of cigarette smoke but compared to what Dani had smelled on the third floor, she welcomed the despised scent of tobacco like it was an old friend. "What do we know? What are they anyway? Fucking zombies or something?"

Raven glanced at Em. "Sorry, I didn't mean…"

Em didn't respond.

"Okay girls," Darryl said, wiping the shine of leftover beer off his chin. "It's time we made some concrete plans. There must be another way out of this shithole. Suggestions?"

"There's a back door," Raven said. "But the only way to reach it if you're on the second floor without going downstairs, is to go back up to the third floor and access the stairs from there. We've been meaning to get the access door on this level fixed for a while. With the Burn, it was just another job that kept getting pushed back."

Raven looked at Em, perhaps wondering if she wanted

to jump in and take it from there. When Em didn't respond, Raven kept talking.

"So right now, it's either the first floor or the third floor to access the back stairs and the fire exit. The electrician's blocked off the first floor, we know that. Creed's locked into the office on the third floor but none of that matters anyway, because the access door to the stairs is locked. We don't usually open it until about ten minutes before we open. Guess where the keys are right now?"

"Office, "Dani said.

"Yep."

Darryl groaned. "That's great. That's just great. We really are trapped in here."

Chiara sat down on the red couch, holding the beer can on her lap with both hands. "Even if we make it out of the Academy, what then? Where are we supposed to go? Christ, why did I have to laugh at all those conspiracy theory nuts who were building hatching shelters in their backyards? That was months ago – think how ready they'll be for this."

"We'll figure out the details later," Darryl said. "But we gotta get out. I for one, am not sticking around in here with two of those things running around."

Raven flicked a tiny avalanche of ash into an empty beer can. "This is happening all over the world, isn't it? Those things, those..."

"Grinners," Dani said, still staring out the window.

"Yeah, grinners. Well, those grinners are everywhere, in every country all over the world. Christ, that's a sobering thought. Isn't it?"

Em, still standing by the pool table, rolled the cue ball back and forth over the baize. "What am I supposed to tell my mother? She wanted me to call her as soon as Creed came back. What do I do now?"

"Didn't you say your mom was stuck in the house with your stepdad?" Chiara asked. "And that he was a...you know?"

"Yeah," Em said, letting the cue ball roll towards the corner pocket. "She is. And he is. I'm too frightened to call. If she doesn't pick up..."

Slowly, she climbed onto the pool table, pushing the balls away and lying on her back.

"I'm tired."

Raven glanced at the TV and watched the Loop segment about the Halfway Dilemma. "Maybe we'll get something new on TV now that it's here. A crumb of useful information, is that too much to ask? They need to tell us we can beat this thing. We've got reserve troopers, fake cops, civilian volunteer squads. We can beat this thing, right?"

She looked at the others. Dani felt the desperation in Raven's voice and couldn't make eye contact.

Chiara shook her head. "There are a helluva lot more grinners than there are reserve troopers, fake cops and civilian whatevers. How about we concentrate on what we can do for ourselves, huh? We could try to make a run for one of the skyscrapers. Vanderbilt, Park Avenue – people have been snapping up rental space on the higher floors for months. Maybe, just maybe, they're letting people inside, helping them get off the ground. If we can get there quick enough..."

"Oh sure," Darryl said, giving Chiara a mock round of applause for all of Manhattan to hear. "The rich people who've bought hiding space in the Vanderbilt are just going to open up their expensive sanctuaries to all the peasants."

Chiara scowled at Darryl.

Em was still lying on the pool table, staring up at the

jagged cracks on the drywall. "I don't know," she said. "I don't know what to do."

Dani slammed her beer down on the window ledge.

"We have to kill them. We have to kill them both. If we do that, we can hide out in the Academy."

Em swung her long legs over the side of the pool table. She stared at the others, especially Dani.

"Talking about killing my brother?"

Dani took off her glasses, letting Em see her eyes. She had to believe that Dani was serious. "He's not your brother anymore."

"Yeah," Darryl said, giving Dani the thumbs up. "Good thinking babe. We can't afford to be sentimental here. Grinner lives don't matter shit."

Em stared at the floor.

"You want to be in charge mister man? You wanna kill my brother and the electrician and then hide out in my place until it's safe to leave? Okay then, how about you earn it? We ain't gonna do shit without a weapon right?"

Darryl shrugged. "You saying you got one?"

"I got one," Em said. "There's a gun downstairs, for emergencies only. It's behind the bar, top drawer, next to the framed picture of Dave Grohl."

"Who?"

"Not the point, is it? You gonna earn the right to talk like a big man? You gonna go downstairs and risk getting yourself killed?"

Raven sat down beside Em on the edge of the pool table. "Em. You understand what they're saying, don't you? You're sure about this?"

"No," Em said, her eyes still locked on Darryl. "I'm not sure, but everyone else seems to be. That much I can tell."

"Ever use this gun before?" Darryl asked.

Raven shook her head. "Nope. We've never had reason to."

Darryl's eyes glazed over for a second. Then the devilish grin was back, the one that a fourteen-year-old Dani Pellerino, along with almost every other girl in school, had been unable to resist.

"I'll do it," he said.

LOOP 8 - THE HALFWAY DILEMMA

Excerpts taken from street interviews.

Melbourne, Australia.
  Interviewee: Dolores Ritchie, 58. Veterinary nurse.

INTERVIEWER: Dolores, are you aware of the Halfway Dilemma?

DOLORES RITCHIE: Yeah I am. That's what you call it when someone's had the Burn for a while, they've been experiencing mental difficulties, and you're not sure if they're the same person they were before. I understand the situation only too well.

INTERVIEWER: You've got personal experience of HD?

DOLORES RITCHIE: Yeah. I live with my partner Katie in Richmond, and to tell you the truth, I have no idea who's in control anymore. When she looks at me there's this ummm, weird thing that passes between us. This strange moment where there's a complete lack of intimacy with the person I know and love more than anyone else in the world. It's not there all the time, but it's happening more and more these days. Sometimes, when I turn around in bed and she's just lying there looking at me, I wonder who's in there. Is it still Katie?

Cut to...

Tokyo, Japan.
Interviewee: Hina Takahashi, 17. Student at Kyoto University.
(English subtitles provided)

HINA TAKAHASHI: Yes I know what HD is. It's happening right now to Toshiro, my youngest brother. He's only eight and for the past week and a half, he's been sitting in the corner of his bedroom at night, peeling and peeling, always doing it when he thinks no one's looking. But there are cameras in there now. My dad put them in, pinhole surveillance cameras, really expensive to buy. And last night...

Hina chews on his lower lip.

INTERVIEWER: Please continue.

HINA TAKAHASHI: Last night, my dad tied him up.

Hina looks at the camera, tries to smile.

HINA TAKAHASHI: It's for his own protection, I swear! We're not bad people or anything like that. We have to restrain him because he doesn't understand what he's doing to himself. Or rather what *it's* doing to him. Toshiro didn't complain when Dad tied him up and that's weird because Toshiro is the biggest crybaby I've ever known. But he didn't cry once, not even when Dad explained that it was for his own good. There was just this weird look on my brother's face. Like he didn't know any of us.

Cut to...

Santiago, Chile.
   Interviewee: Martin Rojas, 39. Lecturer (University of Chile).
   (Subtitles provided)

INTERVIEWER: Martin, you claim you're at the halfway stage now. Is that correct?

MARTIN ROJAS: Yes, that's right. I've even had to take time off work. Anyone who knows me knows that isn't like me at all – I don't take sick days, not ever if I can help it. But I can't ignore it and the truth is that I'm not feeling like myself anymore. Every day I'm losing long stretches of time. Sometimes I can't account for up to three hours and it's as if that part of the day didn't happen for me. It's quite upsetting, I can assure you.

INTERVIEWER: Like blackouts?

MARTIN ROJAS: I don't know what to call it. The doctors aren't too sure either, but it feels like something is taking me over, pushing me out of my own consciousness like I don't belong there. It sounds crazy. I do my best to fight it by wearing the gloves to stop me picking at my face, but when I snap out of these episodes, the gloves are off and there I am on the floor, surrounded by piles of discarded skin. A couple of times I've even found myself in the garden, lying...face down...in...the grass.

Martin's eyes glaze over.

INTERVIEWER: Martin? Martin can you hear me?

8

Darryl had the gun. Now all he had to do was get back upstairs.

Dani watched from the second floor, leaning over the chrome railing as far as she could without tipping over the edge. Her heart was thumping. She didn't know why she was there. None of the others had come out; they were waiting back in the green room with cigarettes, alcohol and the Loop. So why was Dani there? Why did she feel the need to watch over Darryl? Was it due to some lingering husband-wife connection that she hadn't fully severed, or was it because she knew how much they needed that gun?

Darryl's size eleven feet tiptoed away from the bar. With the gun hanging at his side, he approached the lower stairs whilst walking over the old, creaky Academy floor like it was a frozen lake in the spring thaw. It was almost comical. Darryl, one of life's loudest walkers, doing his best to be quiet. Dani couldn't help but be reminded of all those Friday and Saturday nights he'd returned home at three o'clock in the morning, drunk and horny. Sounded like King

Kong coming upstairs every time, asking Dani if she was awake and making sure that she was.

So far, so good. There'd been no sign of the electrician anywhere. Darryl had left the green room in pretty good spirits, but as soon as he was on the upper staircase, his walk had begun to resemble that of someone trudging through an underwater minefield. Every little whisper of noise had his head turning in this direction, that direction, searching for the source of movement.

But the grinner was gone. With any luck it had opened up the front door and walked outside onto Bank Street and beyond. But it was too early to start celebrating yet and besides, they still had Creed to deal with. That wasn't going to be easy, not least because killing Creed would be like killing a part of Em. And boy, would she let everyone know about it.

Now that Darryl had the Glock, there was a little swagger in his step again. Darryl McBride knew guns. He kept a Glock 19 at home, as well as a Browning rifle and a drawer full of exotic daggers, some real mean-looking ones with the serrated edges. Protection, that's how he'd always justified the McBride arsenal to anyone who thought he was a bit over the top. Chiara, on the other hand, called it over-compensation. Darryl had small penis issues, she said. Dani, for her part, never confirmed or denied the allegation.

Darryl saw his wife waiting at the balcony. He gave her a thumbs up, accompanied by a jubilant shit-eating grin.

Dani could see it in his eyes. *You're there. Of course you are, you're the only one who came out to watch me. You're my wife and I'm your husband. Till death do us part Dani my love.*

Was he right?

"No, no, no," Dani whispered. They needed the gun, that's all.

Darryl stopped at the foot of the stairs. Now that he was on the brink of safety, he opened his mouth as if to say something to Dani. But the words were interrupted by a thudding noise from elsewhere on the first floor. Sounded like a door slamming shut, but it was hard to tell where it was coming from.

Footsteps. That was unmistakable. Footsteps, slapping off the hard floor with a strange, offbeat rhythm that was speeding up by the second.

A shape appeared in the corner of the room. Because she had a bird's eye view of the dancefloor, Dani saw it coming before Darryl.

"Look out!"

The electrician's elastic grin widened as it hurried across the floor, reaching for Darryl with long, crooked arms like branches.

"lurvyoooorrr."

Darryl gasped. He retreated instantly, tripping over the first step of the lower staircase and toppling onto his hands and knees. He crawled upstairs, head twisted over his shoulder so that he didn't lose sight of the grinner. He still had the gun, but showed no sign that he was about to use it.

"Shoot it!" Dani yelled. "Darryl. Kill it."

Darryl kept crawling upstairs.

Dani winced. This was a wasted opportunity to get rid of one of those things. Why wasn't Darryl taking advantage of it? She thought of all the endless weekends that he'd dragged her to the shooting range, slowly but surely becoming one of those uptight city guys who thought it was cool to prepare for the collapse of civilization by becoming a crack shot. But this wasn't a paper target anymore. The best shooting ranges in the world couldn't prepare Darryl for what was chasing him.

He was halfway up the lower staircase, still on his hands and knees. Still gasping for breath.

The electrician came to a halt at the foot of the stairs. It stared at Darryl, who by now had reached the landing in between the two sets of stairs leading up to the second floor. Darryl's back was pushed up against the wall, his eyes bulging as he waited for the electrician to make the next move.

The grinner's floppy blond hair was damp, either with sweat or pus. It tilted its head to the side, stiff and bird-like.

"*lurvyooorr, allyoooorwaawwnt.*"

It reached for Darryl, dagger-knuckles fully extended. The forefinger and thumb on both hands snapped open and shut, like two hungry chicks begging for nourishment.

"*munnneeee, allyooorrrwawwnt.*"

At last, Darryl raised the gun and tried to point the barrel at the grinner. Both arms shook, as if caught in the grip of a seizure.

"Get the fuck away from me!" he said, sweat pouring into his eyes. "I'll do you man, I'll fucking do you, I swear to God."

The electrician raised its leg off the ground, touching and probing the edge of the first step with its foot.

Darryl fired off a single round. Miss. Another shot followed, another miss. He looked at his shuddering limbs as if they'd betrayed him.

"What the fuck?"

The electrician was still, as if processing the explosive sound of the two gunshots.

"Screw this," Darryl said.

His fingers opened up, releasing the Glock. The pistol hit the stairs with a defeated thud and Darryl, whose face was covered in dead skin, resumed his frantic crawling on the upper staircase.

"Dani!"

Dani, still leaning over the railing, saw her husband mouth two words at her.

Help me.

The electrician began to walk upstairs.

"*furkmeeeerrr.*"

Dani's knuckles whitened as she gripped the chrome railing. Her heart thumped harder and faster in her chest. What now? Let the electrician catch up with the slowing Darryl and let it rip out his heart? How many nights, lying beside Darryl in bed, had Dani hoped the drunken bastard would choke on his own vomit? Till death do us part, that's what they'd said to one another in the church fifteen years ago. Well, if Darryl died, it was over. No more marriage. No more steel cage. Her old-fashioned folks couldn't argue with death as a reason for separation.

But Dani knew it was all bullshit. It was *her* fault. She could have walked out anytime she wanted, if only she'd had the guts to pack a bag. But she'd allowed disappointment to become a habit and at the same time, she'd become afraid of the alternative. The unknown, once a thrill, had become something scary. If Darryl was a loser, then Dani was the biggest loser of all because she'd stuck around his sorry ass.

She hurried downstairs, her heels skidding at the bottom of the staircase. Darryl was inching towards her, still crawling, reaching, mumbling through the mask of hanging skin on his face.

The electrician was halfway up the lower staircase, its dead, milky gaze fixed upon the married couple.

Dani realized the grinner was close to where Darryl had dropped the gun.

"DANI! What the hell are you doing?"

Dani glanced behind her and saw Chiara, Em and Raven, on the upper balcony. They were leaning over the chrome barrier she'd vacated seconds earlier.

"Leave him!" her sister yelled. "Get up here. Now!"

Dani didn't have time to argue. She raced past Darryl, hurrying over to the abandoned Glock.

"Dani!" Chiara screamed. "Get upstairs!"

Dani crouched down and picked up the gun. Her finger slid naturally over the trigger as if there was a magnetic pull at work.

The grinner watched Dani with a cold, dispassionate eye. As Dani returned its stare, she couldn't help but imagine what he'd once been. The electrician was a plain-looking man, somewhere in between thirty and forty years old. Martin or Mark, wasn't it? Probably had a girlfriend or wife. Did they have kids? One? Two? Kids weren't immune to the Burn, although even the mainstream media outlets, in a rare act of consideration for others, had avoided showing too many images of Burn kids on TV or online. That was too much of a stark reminder for people. It suggested that the future of the human race was in doubt.

"muneeeee, allyooorrrwawwwnt."

It quickened its pace. Instinct took over and Dani hurried over to the top of the lower staircase, pulled her left knee in and lashed out with the flat of her shoe. The kick went high and landed flush, hitting the electrician in the face, stunning it and knocking it off balance. Its body shuddered, but it didn't go down.

Dani gritted her teeth and kicked again, to the chest this time. At the same time, she raised the Glock, ready to blow its head clean off but there was no need to squeeze the trigger. The electrician was already crashing back downstairs after the second kick, bashing its head off the steps as it returned to the first floor.

Dani stood at the top of the stairs, feeling like time had stopped. She watched as the grinner sat up quickly on the floor, looking up at Dani. The grin was still wide, still carved onto its face. It reached its arms towards her.

"*lurvyoooorrr.*"

Dani grabbed Darryl by the arm, picking him up off the floor. Darryl grunted like he didn't know what was going on or where he was, but his legs still worked and he picked up the pace to match the speed of his wife.

They hurried up the upper staircase.

"Dani!" Chiara hollered, running to the top the stairs. "Quick. It's coming."

Dani didn't look behind her. She didn't want to see that white-eyed thing lumbering at high speed, reaching out with those snapping jaw-like fingers. Nonetheless, she could hear the clunky rhythm of its bare feet slapping off the stairs. Could hear its choked voice calling out to her.

"*allyooorwawwnt!*"

Chiara rushed down to her sister, almost losing her balance at the halfway point of the staircase. She met Dani and offered her hand.

"C'mon!"

Dani tucked the Glock into the waist of her pants and reached for Chiara. With her spare hand, she dragged the shellshocked figure of Darryl behind her.

LOOP 9 - THE CLEAN

Interview with Brendan Cosmo, 45. Chartered accountant from Dublin, Ireland.

It's a beautiful spring evening in Dublin. Brendan and Annie Divlin, an interviewer from RTÉ, are sitting on a bench in Phoenix Park, located a few kilometers west of the city center. It's close to sunset and the horizon is awash with yellow and orange and pink as the sun slowly disappears behind a vast wall of trees. In the distance, not too far from the bench where Brendan and Annie are chatting, a small herd of wild deer is grazing.

ANNIE DIVILIN: Brendan, you had the Burn for about three weeks but look at you now. There's no trace of it on you whatsoever. You're a symbol of hope, aren't you?

Brendan smiles at the young, female reporter. Annie is heavily made up, concealing about ninety percent of the Burn on her face and neck. Brendan's craggy skin is completely unblemished.

BRENDAN COSMO: Well I don't feel like a symbol of hope to tell you the truth Annie. Believe it or not, ummm, it's not all sunshine and rainbows when you're one of the Clean. Between life at home with my family and being poked and prodded twenty-four hours a day in the lab, I'm starting to feel a little frustrated. I don't say this lightly, but sometimes I think I was better off when I had the Burn. At least I was like everyone else, you know?

ANNIE DIVILIN: Can you tell us about the difficulties you're facing Brendan?

BRENDAN COSMO: Guilt. That's the worst of it alright. I feel guilty every day because I don't have the Burn and both my children have it. My wife has it too. I look at them across the table during dinner, knowing full well that I'm out of the quicksand they're still sinking in. And there's nothing I can do about it. Jesus, I can only hope to God that whatever genetic ingredient spared me is alive in them and that it'll show itself sooner rather than later. There doesn't seem to be any rhyme or reason to it Annie. Why me? Was it something I did? Something I didn't do? Is it all down to luck in the end? I don't know.

ANNIE DIVILIN: Sounds like you're experiencing something like survivor's guilt.

BRENDAN COSMO: I don't know much about survivor's guilt. But here's what I do know and again, this isn't easy to say out loud. People I've known for years, liked for years and loved for years, they look at me as if I've betrayed them somehow. Nobody says anything of course, but I see it in their eyes. There's a coldness that wasn't there before. Tell you the truth Annie, I think I really am happier in the lab when the white coats are poking me with their needles. At least there I know where I stand.

Brendan tries to laugh but it's unconvincing.

BRENDAN COSMO: Sorry for all the negativity. This was supposed to be a positive news story wasn't it?

ANNIE DIVILIN: You're grand Brendan. It's alright, really.

Brendan nods and points towards something about fifty meters down the path from the bench. It's a cocoon, a white, shapeless blob sealed in a glass tank. The identity ticket attached to the side flaps in the breeze.

BRENDAN COSMO: Would you look at that? What's the world coming to when that's a normal, everyday sight?

Annie glances at the cocoon.

ANNIE DIVILIN: Sorry about that Brendan. It's hard to find somewhere to set up outside where there isn't at least one of them. You know?

BRENDAN COSMO: Aye, I know. I guess I should feel some measure of relief when I see those things, but the truth is I don't feel anything. Well that's not quite true. There's dread because I'm aware that *that* might happen to Amy and my children, Zach and Cathy. And whenever I think of that, of having to watch the gardaí put a tank over them, and then being left alone in the house with them, I ask myself, Jesus...who's really the lucky one?

9

"Hurry up!" Em said, slamming the green room door shut and locking it after everyone was inside.

Chiara grabbed Dani by the arm, wrenching her away from Darryl. Darryl, who'd been leaning on Dani's shoulder for support, went down like a ton of bricks. He collapsed face-first onto the floor and stayed there. Besides a weak grunt, he barely registered the fall.

"What the fuck were you thinking?" Chiara yelled. Her angry breath steamed up Dani's glasses. "You put your life on the line for him of all people? Are you crazy Dani?"

Dani stood there, listening as Chiara went on about how she shouldn't have been there in the first place, about how she should have left Darryl to die on the stairs. And so on. Dani nodded listlessly and looked at her hands. They weren't shaking. Even after what had just happened out there, they weren't shaking. Calm was a good place to be right now anyway. Dani knew her sister was too fired up to reason with and that Chiara would stay hot until she'd let it all out. That's just how it was. Even as she approached forty years of age, Chiara was still the resident Pellerino firecracker and that was saying something when it came to the Pellerinos, a family full of hotheads. Whenever her older sister went off at her like this, Dani would often think back to the summer of '96 when a teenage Chiara had caught her Fabio-wannabe boyfriend Dario kissing Susie Bannon, a skinny bitch (according to Chiara) who lived two houses down from the Pellerinos. Chiara had let poor Dario have it that day in the middle of the road, whipping him on the back with a 9-iron that she'd stolen from the old man's golf bag. Everyone in the neighborhood had watched from the comfort of their living room windows, lapping up the free entertainment. Dani did too, watching from her bedroom window as Chiara beat the crap out of Dario, a boy she'd called 'the one' only the day before.

Chiara couldn't be reached with words when she was this far gone.

"After what he did to you?" Chiara yelled for the tenth time. "You run downstairs and put yourself within arm's reach of that thing? To protect Darryl fucking McBride of all people? Why Dani? You almost gave me a heart attack."

Dani shrugged. "I..."

"Fuck him!" Chiara said. "His life didn't amount to nothing and he dragged you down with him. And you know what really fucking gets me every time sis? You wanna know? It's that you let him! You had everything going for you – talent, good looks, brains, and you let him pull you under."

Those last five words were a dealbreaker.

Dani, the quiet Pellerino, pushed Chiara, forcing her sister halfway across the green room. Chiara recovered her balance and stood rigid like a mannequin. Her mouth hung open as if to speak, but no words came out.

"I know I let him!" Dani screamed. She charged forward,

and for a split second she even raised the Glock as if to point it at her sister. But she didn't and instead, Dani lowered the pistol to her side and tucked it in tight to her leg.

The red mist cleared a little. Her voice was calm again.

"You don't need to tell me Chiara. You love to blame Darryl for everything, but it wasn't just Darryl. It was me. I put up with it. I stayed."

Chiara's eyes began to fill up. She held out her hands, reaching for her sister. "Dani, I'm sorry."

Dani backed away, glancing down at her husband who was now sitting cross-legged on the floor, head buried in his hands. She imagined pointing the barrel at the top of his head and squeezing the trigger. Bang. Instant divorce. And yet it would change nothing.

Darryl slowly pushed himself back to his feet. He touched the wreckage of his blistered face, dabbing at it gently like it was about to fall off.

"I'm okay," he said. "I'm okay."

"Hey," Raven said, pointing at the TV. "Look at this you guys. I think they're showing something new on the Loop. That's not a rerun, is it?"

Dani, along with everyone else, turned towards the TV. Raven was right. This was the post-hatching news. The public were sending in footage they'd uploaded to the Loop online, most likely to share information about what was happening in their part of the world. Most of the images were rough, but they painted a clear enough picture of what was going on. Not that any of the five people inside the green room needed the Loop to know what was going on. Dani saw the names of all the places at the bottom of the screen: Sydney. Tianjin. Mexico City. Cairo. London. And more. People being chased on the streets by naked, white-eyed grinners, caught, killed, and having their hearts ripped out and eaten. There were no censors to conceal the worst of the footage.

Dani felt a hand graze her shoulder. She spun around and her blood stopped in her veins.

"Thank you darling," Darryl croaked. He was talking through a paper mache face, his mouth half-buried under a sheet of cocoon whiteness. "I don't know what happened to me on the stairs back there. I just froze. It's like this thing in my head, it won't let me..."

He shook his head.

"But I'm alright now. Here, I'll hold onto the gun while we figure this thing out."

Dani was so repulsed by the sight of Darryl that she didn't resist as he gently removed the Glock out of her hands. He kept telling her he was alright. Their hands brushed against one another's at the exchange and Dani screamed inside as she felt Darryl's skin, damp and soft, like a sponge.

"We need to organize," Darryl said, sluggishly checking the magazine for ammo.

"Organize?" Dani said, inching away from her husband.

Darryl nodded. "We have to get rid of those things. We're the humans here, not them and that means we've got the smarts on our side. They're brainless monsters for God's sake – you've heard them trying to talk. How hard can it be?"

"Who died and made you leader?" Chiara asked.

A loud thump at the door made everyone jump.

The electrician's ghoulish face was pressed up tight against one of the glass panels. He was staring into the green room, hitting the door with both hands in a patient, maddening rhythm that sounded like it was just warming up.

"allyoorrrwawwwnt."

And then, Creed's blood-soaked face appeared in the vacant panel. Now there were two sets of dead eyes staring at the five people inside.

"muneeee, furkmeeer."

"Creed!" Em said.

"How the hell did he get out?" Chiara asked. "Please tell me he didn't break down a locked door because that's not what I need to hear right now."

Em began to walk towards the door. Creed's jerky head movement followed his sister's approach.

"lurrvyooowrr."

"It's not Creed," Raven yelled, stepping in front of Em. She stretched her arms out to the sides, transforming her tiny frame into a human roadblock. "It's not him. Snap out of it Em."

"No," Darryl said, staring at Creed and the electrician in horror. His voice was shaking. His entire body was shaking from head to toe. "Oh God, no. Fuck this. I won't die like this, not here, no fucking way. Not like this. They're not going to pull my heart out of my body and fucking EAT IT."

He paced the room, sweat dripping off his head.

"Get the fuck out of here you freaks!"

With his spare hand, Darryl was peeling frantically at the loose skin that stubbornly clung onto his neck. When he realized what he was doing, he backed away to the wall and looked around the room like he'd just woken up from a nightmare.

"What's happening to me?"

"Darryl," Dani said in a firm, but reassuring voice. "You need to calm down. Okay? Take a deep breath, you're all over the place."

There was an explosion of breaking glass. Dani gasped as she saw Creed's arm reaching through a hole in the panel, his long dark fingers snapping at thin air. Shards of glass trickled off the back of his hand, spilling onto the green room floor.

"*furkmeeerrr.*"

Dani felt a tremendous force pulling her backwards towards the window. It wasn't instinct, it was Chiara. She had Dani by the arm, leading her as far away from the door as she possibly could. Raven steered a reluctant Em to the same spot.

Darryl was by now in the middle of the room, eyes closed, spinning around slowly in a drunken daze. He tapped the barrel of the gun off his temple. "What's happening to me man? I don't feel good. This thing it's…"

He swatted the Glock at thin air, as if a plague of locusts had attacked him all of a sudden.

"Get off!" he screamed. "Get away from me!"

Creed's arm continued to explore the other side of the door. Dani didn't like how the grinner's hand was closing in on the door handle, especially with the key still hanging off the lock. She wanted to believe that the mechanics of unlocking a door were beyond the grinners' mental capacity. But she couldn't let go of another thought. What if something of the host's memory had been retained post-transformation? And what if those memories could be accessed whenever required? The human Creed knew how to unlock a door. Did that mean the grinner version knew?

She watched those long fingers closing in on the key.

"Jesus!" Chiara said, taking a step forward. "You guys see that? It's like he's looking for the key or something."

"I don't know," Raven answered. "Can he do that?"

Chiara stepped forward. "Fuck this. I'm not waiting to find out."

She hurried across the room, her feet like claps of thunder. By now, Creed's wandering hand was inches away and a smidge to the left of the jackpot.

Chiara's sudden burst of movement made Darryl drop to his knees. "No! Don't touch me. Don't fucking touch me!"

He narrowed his eyes, swatting the air above his head with the Glock. Chiara hurried past, paying no attention to her brother-in-law. She reached the door and kicked Creed's arm to the side. Then she pulled the key out of the lock.

"Yes! Got it."

Creed's arm shot out, grabbing her by the shoulder.

"Chiara!" Dani yelled. "Get out of there."

Creed's voice rose about two octaves due to the excitement of the catch. "*allyoorwawnt*." He began to reel Chiara in, dragging her towards the door.

"Chiara!"

"Stay there Dani."

Chiara gritted her teeth. She reached for the hand on her shoulder, grabbed the three middle fingers and began to pull them backwards, manipulating the joints until there was a loud snapping noise that could be heard clearly inside the green room.

"Fuck you asshole!"

Creed didn't yell out in pain, but he did let go of Chiara's shoulder. The arm slid back through the gap in defeat.

A second later, the grinners started hammering on the door again. They were hitting it much harder than before, as if they really did want to break it down.

Chiara backed away slowly, covering her ears with both hands. She turned around and took off in a sprint, hurrying back towards Dani and the others at the window.

Darryl flinched as Chiara's shadow fell upon him. "Get away! Get away from me."

He jumped to his feet and cried out for all of New York

to hear. "Fuck you, you bastards from Hell. I'm not going to die like this. No one's ripping my heart out! No one's ripping my heart out!"

Darryl screamed. There was a loud crack inside the green room as he squeezed the trigger.

Dani was silent as she watched her big sister fall like a toppled statue. She saw Darryl standing over Chiara, shaking like a man who'd just gone skinny dipping in the Arctic Ocean. The Glock slipped out of his fingers and fell to the floor. Darryl took a backwards step, pulling off his hoodie and throwing it across the room like he was a stripper. All the while he cried out that he was melting. That he didn't mean it. That he was melting. That he didn't mean it. He sat down, cross-legged on the floor again and began to chip away at the loose skin on his chest.

With a hollow sensation in the pit of her stomach, Dani sprinted over, dropping down beside her sister. Chiara was flat on her back, rapid-blinking eyes staring up at the ceiling. Her mouth was frozen in a large O-shape as if she'd stopped in the middle of a word. But there were no words, only the sight of Chiara's chest rising and falling at a tremendous speed.

Em and Raven stood over the sisters, but they might as well have been miles away for all Dani cared.

"Chiara," Dani said, cradling her sister's head in her arms. She barely recognized her voice, which was going up and down in pitch in time with Chiara's distressed breathing. "Can you hear me? Hold on, okay? Don't you go anywhere. Don't you dare! We're going to fix this, it's not bad."

Chiara's focus came down from the ceiling. She found the eyes of her younger sister and then winced at a sudden explosion of pain.

"I..."

They locked hands together.

Dani stared at the blood gathering around Chiara's chest. There was so much of it she didn't even know where the bullet hole was located. Dani's arms and legs spasmed. She was trying to hold it together for Chiara but it felt like she was dying too.

Chiara tried to talk again. "I..."

"Don't," Dani said, putting a finger over Chiara's lips and then removing it quickly as if she was afraid of suffocating her sister. "Save your strength. It's not as bad as I thought, okay? I've had a look and it's not bad Chiara. So just stay with me, okay? Just focus on staying awake and looking at me."

Raven was down on her knees, trying to press a towel over the wound. She was crying.

The grinners were still throwing their weight against the door. There was no doubt – the assault had intensified since the shooting. Was the blood exciting them? Could they smell it?

Chiara's body rattled as if shocked by a defibrillator.

"No!" Dani screamed. "Chiara. Please."

She squeezed tight on Chiara's hand, cursing herself for not knowing what to do in this situation. The fingers of her other hand, covered in blood, caressed Chiara's cheek and she rejected the notion that her sister was dying in front of her. Pellerino sisters, best friends for life. For *life*. That included old age, two grumpy old Italian bitches sitting on a porch somewhere, drinking tea, complaining about the speed of the traffic going past the house.

Chiara was not shrinking before Dani's eyes. Not her hero. Her big sister.

"We have a gig to do," Dani said, knowing that it was a ridiculous thing to say. "And I can't do it without you."

But Chiara was already gone.

Time stopped inside the green room. Dani held the lifeless body of her sister in her arms. She couldn't move, couldn't breathe. And then, a blurry noise exploded from somewhere else inside the room. Dani heard the screams behind her – screams? What was going on? What was *that* noise? Sounded like Raven and Em, still a million miles away but close. They were shouting, saying her name, telling her to get up off the floor. Something about the door.

Dani felt a strong pair of hands scooping her up off the carpet. Those hands were dragging her away from her sister and doing it in a hurry.

Dani reached for Chiara.

"No!"

"She's gone." Raven's voice cried out. "Dani she's gone." That voice was clear, like a rope pulling Dani back to the present.

Raven continued to steer Dani towards the door. "C'mon. They kicked the door open, they're in here, and we need to get out."

The fog in Dani's mind began to lift. Creed and the electrician? They were inside the dressing room?

She looked left and right.

And then she saw them.

The grinners were down on their knees, one on either side of Chiara. In unison, they curled their fingers into tight fists, extending the dagger knuckles and aiming the tips at the dead woman's chest.

Dani's legs gave way. She screamed. If not for Raven and Em she would have collapsed altogether or maybe she would have gone back into the green room and fought for her sister. But Em and Raven had a solid grip on Dani and they dragged her through the open doorway. Dani went numb, listening to the sound of her sister being carved open fading into the distance.

There was a flicker of movement behind the three women as they made their getaway. The wretched shape of Darryl followed them. He shadowed their retreat, moving like a Saturday night drunk chasing the last cab down the street.

LOOP 10 - CARNAGE

Fort William, Scotland.

A school gymnasium. Faint orange light trickles down from the ceiling. The floor, decorated with the usual multicolored court markings, is covered in long trails of a blackish red fluid.

A camera is filming from the back row of the seating area surrounding the gym. The view is pretty much like that of a lone spectator looking down on a basketball game.

Screams.

The silhouettes on the gym floor, awkward and ape-like, hurry back and forth with boundless enthusiasm. Some run. Some crawl. More screams. Some of the screamers run for the stairs that lead up to the seating area, close to where the cameraperson is hiding. These runners are promptly cut off by more ape-shadows that flood through the fire exit like water through a broken dam.

A child's voice narrates over the footage. The boy speaks quietly, doing just enough to be heard.

BOY: I'm uploading this to the Loop. Can you see? They're here in the gym, hundreds of them. Hundreds of hatchlings.

A pause.

BOY: There's no way out. They've cut off all the exits I know of. They must have heard one of the babies crying or something – that's how they knew we were in here. It must be that, I don't know what else it could be. Dad said that three hundred people took sanctuary in the school and I think most of them are already dead. I don't know where Dad is. Mr. Thompson, the headmaster here, he's dead for sure. I ran over him on my way to the stairs. Danny, his son and a boy I go to school with here, was still alive when I saw him running towards the fire exit.

My name is John Campbell. I'm twelve.

The camera zooms in on the far corner of the gym. It's a fuzzy picture but clear enough that the viewer can see a silver-haired woman of about sixty being cornered by four male hatchlings. The woman's hands are up in surrender as she backs off towards the wall.

She says something, then starts peeling the skin off her face like it's a race. It's as if she's trying to convince the hatchlings that she's one of them.

Her plan doesn't work.

10

Raven held onto Dani's arm as they made their way down the second-floor corridor. Dani's legs moved on autopilot, not because she willed them to. She couldn't feel anything from the neck down. Felt like she was floating.

"Em," Raven called out. "Hey, are you listening to me for Christ's sake? I said where are we going?"

Em, who was leading the way, stopped and turned around. She wiped away the tear tracks staining both sides of her face.

"What do you want from me?"

"I just want to know where we're going," Raven said. "What we're doing here. Why didn't we go downstairs for a starter? Are we going out the fire exit or what?"

"Out?" Em said, squinting her eyes. "Out where? Got a helicopter waiting on the roof or something Raven? Got an uber at the back door? Why do you think I've got all the answers anyway? You tell me where we're going."

Dani felt like a limp rag, caught in Raven's grip. She could hear their voices but she wasn't listening. Not really.

"Are we staying in the Academy?" Raven asked. "That's

all I'm asking for Christ' sake – it's a perfectly reasonable thing to ask. Are we really staying in here with those fucking monsters running around ripping out hearts and eating them?"

There was an expression of blank disappointment on Em's face. "Monsters? Really Raven?"

Raven cursed under her breath. She finally let go of Dani's arm. "I'm sorry Em, I didn't mean that. You know I thought the world of Creed too, right?"

"I know."

They were silent for a moment.

"Did you see it?" Em whispered. "What he did?"

Raven nodded. "I saw it. I'll never forget it for as long as I live but hey, you gotta remember something Em. It's not Creed. I keep saying that I know, but you gotta remember – it's just something that looks like him. He didn't do that to Chiara."

Em exhaled out loud, seemingly on the brink of exhaustion. "What if he's still in there somewhere?"

"No. You can't think like that."

Dani leaned her back against the chrome railing. She closed her eyes, waiting for the feeling of weightlessness to pass.

"You only saw Creed the big joker," Em said to Raven. "The comedian with the soul of a clown. He always thought he was so much funnier than he was, right? That was Creed as an adult, but man you should have seen him when he was a little boy. Softest kid ever. Scared of everything, that was Creed. We shared a bedroom when we were kids and if the floorboards so much as creaked, he'd throw back the covers and go take shelter in Mom and Dad's bed. Stay there all night. He thought it was monsters creeping upstairs to get us. I used to tell him there was no such thing as monsters.

What did I know? But he was a good kid. Had a big heart you know? He was the sort of kid who'd chase flies around the house, following them in and out of each room, running upstairs and downstairs with a cup and an envelope, all so he could do a catch and release. Didn't matter to Creed how long it took. He never swatted a fly in his life. I thought he was crazy, wasting time like that but he'd always say to me, what if it was you Em? What if you suddenly found yourself in the wrong place, surrounded by monsters that couldn't hear you scream? What would you want them to do to you? Set you free or squash your ass up with the world's biggest rolled up newspaper?"

Raven smiled. "Yeah, he was the best."

"I've been playing big sister all my life," Em said. "It becomes a habit."

"Help meeeee. Pleeease...help me."

Heavy footsteps scraped off the floor.

Darryl was gasping for breath as he labored his way down the corridor. He'd been playing catch up ever since they'd left the green room. Most of his clothes had been removed except for a pair of black boxer shorts with a red arrow on the front pointing to the crotch and a caption that read: *Don't Need a Permit for this Gun!*

He leaned up against the wall for support. Half his face was gone, replaced by white cocoon mask. One beady eye shifted left and right, coming to a stop when it landed on Dani.

He reached for her.

"I'm sorry," he said. "I..."

Dani stared at the pathetic remnants of her husband. One moment, she felt nothing and then the next it was like a volcano had gone off inside her. She leaped across the narrow width of the corridor, shoving him to the ground. He was light and soft and fell easily. Dani kicked Darryl's ribs as hard as she could, once, twice, three times, and his body jolted in response. It wasn't enough. She mounted him, her glasses falling off her face as he tried to wriggle free of her weight. He felt liquid soft, mushy. Dani screamed, raining punches down on his face.

Hitting Darryl felt like hitting wet sand.

"You killed her!"

Darryl's body made a strange whistling noise like it was deflating.

"*Noooo. Didn't meeeen it. Not. Yooooo. Bleeeve me, pleeeze.*"

Dani felt a kaiju-esque monster awakening within her. Her inner Godzilla. She was ready to strangle this man. Fuck it, who'd care when people were dying everywhere and getting their hearts ripped out by monsters? It was the perfect time to settle old scores. But Dani's monster was too impatient for violence. She wanted this to last, to draw it out forever and take revenge for Chiara and for the last fifteen years. It had to satisfy. Death was too easy, too quick. So instead of strangling him, Dani grabbed at the loose skin on his body and face, pulling it off with reckless abandon. What a thrill it was. She was literally making the man disappear, once and for all. Right in front of her. Shrinking. Gone.

Darryl's eye, the one that wasn't yet hidden, bulged as Dani unwrapped him.

"How does it feel Darryl?" Dani hissed. "How does it feel? You're going to be one of them. One of *them*!"

"*Stopppp, pleeeeze.*"

"I know you shot her," Dani said. "I know *you* shot her."

"*Noooo…*"

"STOP! Leave him alone."

Dani felt the others dragging her away. She resisted but they managed to pull her back to her feet, steering her away from what was left of her husband who was curled up in a ball on the floor, incoherently mumbling and sobbing to himself.

"Get the fuck off me!" Dani yelled.

She wrestled free of Em and Raven who'd both grabbed an arm each. Dani walked away, grabbing her glasses off the floor. After wiping the lenses down, she glared at the two women who'd interrupted her beatdown.

"He murdered Chiara. He saw his chance back there and took it."

"For God's sake," Raven said. "Look at him Dani. He doesn't know what the hell's going on anymore. He's changing. He's..."

"He's a fucking asshole!" Dani screamed. She felt like the top of her head was about to blow open. "You don't know what he's like Raven. I know, and Chiara knows. What the fuck am I doing here? Why did I bring her here tonight? I'm thirty-five years old and look at me, trying to be a punk rocker on that stage, thinking I'm still eighteen for Christ's sake. Punk? Me? I'm a sell-out. I sold out the last fifteen years of my life because I didn't have the guts to rock the boat. I was worried about disappointing everyone in my family and where the fuck were they tonight? Chiara's the only one who ever believed in me. *Me.* That's why she came here today; she came to see her sister again for the first time in fifteen years. Fuck, I'm so sorry Chiara."

Dani felt a sudden pinch in her right arm. She felt the urge to dig her fingernails deep into her face, to rummage around in search of dead skin. It was hot inside the Academy, like a giant oven turned up to full. She'd feel better, if she peeled just a little.

"No," she said.

Dani turned around, facing the second-floor corridor that led back to the stairs. Back to the green room.

"I can't leave her like that. They're eating my sister like she's a piece of road kill."

"Dani," Raven said. "We can't..."

There was a massive thump at the front door. Sounded like someone had driven their car into the side of the building. It was immediately followed by a man's voice. A voice that shook with terror.

"HELP! LET ME IN. IS ANYONE THERE?"

The women stared at one another, none of them daring to speak.

Three more hits on the door. Once again, it sounded like someone ramming a truck against the building.

"HELP ME!" the man's voice begged. "PLEASE HE..."

The voice shifted an octave higher, making a strangled noise before cutting out altogether. This was followed by a minute of uneasy silence.

"What the hell just happened?" Raven asked.

When the pounding restarted, it was different. It slower for a start; it was patient. This was a familiar maddening thump, something cold and dispassionate, something that all three women had encountered earlier that night.

Thump. Thump. Thump.

"furkmeeeeerr."

"munneeee."

"allyoooorwawwwnt."

"Holy shit," Em said. "How many of them are out there?"

The voices outside the Academy fought to be heard. There were so many, raspy and full of longing, that it was impossible to answer Em's question.

LOOP 11 - THE HEART-EATERS

Emergency news broadcast (uploaded to the Loop Online).

The camera approaches a large table with four people, two seated on either side. We're in some kind of underground bunker with shadowy figures hurrying back and forth at speed, papers in hand, cellphones pressed to their ears.

The walls of the bunker are made of a granite-like stone. A neat row of whiteboards is lined up near the table, displaying multiple sheets of A4 paper, all covered in text and diagrams, as well as graphs and maps.

A bottle of wine sits on the table. Four empty glasses. A tray of sandwiches has been left untouched.

The camera reaches the table and zooms in on Adam Tweed, best known as a political affairs commentator and regular newspaper contributor for the New York Times. There's no loose skin visible on Tweed's face, suggesting that he (or one of his aides) is extremely skilled in makeup. Either that or he's one of the Clean.

———

ADAM TWEED: Good evening ladies and gentleman. Fellow survivors. Welcome to this special broadcast coming to you on the Loop Online.

A pause.

ADAM TWEED: Well, it happened tonight. The cocoons that we've lived alongside for all these months, in our towns and cities and suburbs, have hatched. The question now is, what's hatched? Who or what are these individuals, what do they want and what can we do to help them, as well as help ourselves and stay safe? This special broadcast, coming to you from a secret location near Los Angeles, will try to shed some light on the subject.

Tweed glances at the two men and the woman sitting alongside him.

ADAM TWEED: Joining me for this special broadcast tonight are Former Marine, Staff Sergeant George Gould, along with Nicki Strusser, a philosophy lecturer at Berkeley, and novelist Jim Mann, best known for the Jack Harrison thriller series and his collection of non-fiction essays about social themes in twenty-first century America.

Strusser and Mann acknowledge Tweed and the camera. Gould remains poker-faced, staring into empty space.

ADAM TWEED: Well, how to begin? The reports coming in from above ground are disturbing to say the least. The hatchlings, that's what people seem to be calling them and that's what we'll call them for now, are similar to the people we knew in terms of appearance. That much is clear. The differences however, are startling and quite shocking. Most of us have already observed the physical differences but in terms of behavior, boy have we got ourselves a problem folks. The hatchlings, it would seem, want to eat your heart. As one video blogger said whilst filming a mall massacre in Dayton, Ohio this evening, they're not just heart hungry. They're heart famished.

Tweed turns to Nicki Strusser, an attractive blonde woman of about fifty-five. As well as being a lecturer at Berkeley, she's also an author covering subjects such as philosophy, history, mythology and religion.

ADAM TWEED. Nicki, why the heart?

NICKI STRUSSER: Well, we don't have much to draw upon for comparison Adam, but I guess that's stating the obvious. For me however, Egyptian mythology sprang to mind when I learned about the hatchlings' hunger for the heart. You see in Ancient Egypt, if a human heart was not deemed worthy at judgment it would be eaten by Ammut, an Egyptian demoness, the 'eater of hearts' and 'devourer of the dead'. The owner of the heart would thus become a restless soul, doomed to wander forever without peace. Some depictions also show the unworthy hearts being cast into a lake of fire to be destroyed. No matter how far-fetched it may sound to our modern ears, might we consider the presence of the hatchlings a form of, dare I say it, judgment?

ADAM TWEED: Divine judgment?"

NICKI STRUSSER: I'm not making any definitive statements. What I'm trying to do is to make sense of why it's the heart, drawing upon what I know in terms of historical and mythological tradition. They're not eating our brains, lungs, kidneys or any other organs for that matter. Everything else is left intact. Egyptian mythology is perhaps something to consider because there's nothing obvious in our own culture that explains why it's the heart they want. But let's be honest, we're not sure of anything here. That's a humbling statement I know, but it's true. Despite a tendency amongst some to believe otherwise, we don't even have confirmation that the dust storms caused the Burn. It's the most likely explanation but we just don't know.

Tweed turns to Jim Mann. Mann, 57, is a big man, over 6'2 and at least two hundred and thirty pounds. He's an eternal fidgeter, shifting restlessly in his seat, and threading a pen through the gaps in his fingers.

TWEED: Jim, what do you make of the hatchlings?

JIM MANN: What I want to know Adam old buddy, is whether there's anything of the old mind still there? You know what I mean? The hatchlings sure as hell resemble the people we used to know, but is it just a replication? Are our people still in those bodies? I don't know, but if the hatchlings *are* still classified as human then it's kind of awkward because what we're talking about now is cannibalism. Plain and simple. And nobody likes talking about cannibalism.

ADAM TWEED: *If* we still classify them as human.

NICKI STRUSSER: Yes. And that's a big 'if' at the moment.

JIM MANN: My own feeling is that the 'C' word is something we're going to have to face up to in the coming days. I think the virus, whatever it was that got inside us, triggers something that was already there, our deep-rooted cannibalistic tendencies that we've suppressed or diverted over the years and channeled into other outlets. But it's there, it's always been there. And no matter how slick our innovations, no matter how large our capacity for intellectual and technological growth, it's always there. The desire to devour one another.

NICKI STRUSSER: Cannibalism, as horrific as it is, is certainly less unfamiliar to us than the notion of an extraterrestrial invasion initiated by a global dust storm. Human beings have eaten one another throughout history, out of necessity and for religious or even magical purposes. Some historical societies, such as the Fiji Islanders displayed it proudly, while others have distanced themselves from it. We know that cannibalism was practiced by Stone Age people at the caves of Cheddar Gorge in England where people even made drinking cups out of the skulls. It also occurred in Russia during the famine in the early twentieth century. I believe that cannibalism is associated with a fear of swallowing and being swallowed. It's about a loss of personal identity. A lot of people thought that monsters would come out of the cocoons, and so we thought in terms of *otherness*. But guess what? We recognize their faces, don't we? We see our loved ones in the hatchlings, in these so-called monsters. Personally, I think there's a good chance they're still human.

JIM MANN: They're human alright. And I'm sure we'll find everything intact once we get a few live ones in a lab and start probing around and doing some tests.

ADAM TWEED: George Gould, you're a former marine. You have a different take on this don't you?

Gould speaks with a stern, cutting voice. His accent reeks of the Deep South, most likely Alabama or Mississippi.

GEORGE GOULD: Well it's not Judgment Day, that's for sure. And those killers out there ain't human, at least not anymore. This is an act of war. Now hear me out folks because I'm not trying to be the typical macho military asshole in the room, but I don't believe for one second they're still human. You intellectuals play your word games if you want, but I'm a soldier and I see something different when I look at the situation. Look at them for God's sake, we've all seen the footage on the Loop. This is an attack from an invasive species and this heart-eating business is about one thing and one thing only – dominance. Now I know a little bit about cannibalism too folks and eating your enemy is the most extreme act of dominance there is. It's all about contempt. This is not a mindless enemy we're dealing with here. This is a foreign species, call it alien if you will, and it's extremely intelligent. It's crippled our civilization. It's hijacked our bodies and now it's targeting our most sacred and symbolic of organs, the heart. Whoever our attackers are, take it from an old soldier, they have nothing but contempt for us.

ADAM TWEED: If you're right George, how do we fix it? How do we understand it?

GEORGE GOULD: Personally, I'd rather kick the shit out of it first and understand it later.

ADAM TWEED: But do we have the resources left to do that? Do we even have the manpower to fight back?

Gould hesitates, then signals his unwillingness to answer.

Footage ends.

11

Dani listened to the grinners banging on the door downstairs.

It would hold. It *had* to hold.

She took some comfort in the fact that it had been a tight squeeze bringing the amp through that front door earlier. They'd used the front door instead of the regular load in at the back because according to Larry, the back was reserved for big bands with drums and extensive backlines. Dani had felt aggrieved at the time because she wanted to feel legit, instead of a pay-to-play who'd only secured a gig because the Academy was desperate. But now she was grateful, knowing from experience that the width of the front passageway would help to stem the tide of grinners. Despite all those voices out there, there was probably no more than two of them hitting the door at once. That would buy them some time.

Dani could hear the hunger in their cries. It sounded like the voices of the damned, burning in hellfire, begging for water. That raw longing went through Dani like a hollow-point bullet.

"How do they know we're in here?" Raven asked.

"They don't," Dani said, leaning over the railing, watching the door. The siege leaders were slapping it with that slow, methodical rhythm that she'd heard from Creed and the electrician on the green room door. That patient attack was at odds with the hunger in their voices. It was almost like they were taunting their prey rather than trying to get in.

"You heard that guy a minute ago," Dani said. "The grinners don't know we're in here for sure. They just followed him here and now they're trying their luck."

"Don't know that for sure though," Raven said. "Do we?"

Dani nodded. "We don't know jack shit for sure."

Raven pulled out a cigarette and struggled to light it. When the tip finally glowed red, she inhaled and blew the smoke away from the others.

The door sounded like a bass drum going through a loudspeaker.

"Sounds like they're picking it up a notch," Raven said. "Telling all the grinners in New York that this is where the party's at."

Em joined the others, peering over the edge of the railing. "This night just keeps getting better and better. Doesn't it?"

"Okay," Raven said. "What now?"

Dani wiped the mist off her glasses. She could hear Darryl behind her, still curled up in a tight ball on the floor. His voice was different. He sounded like a young child singing a lullaby to himself.

Raven lifted her t-shirt at the waist, revealing the handle of the Glock tucked into her pants. "Didn't think I'd leave this in the green room, did you?"

She removed the gun and held it aloft.

"What do you say ladies? I say we don't go down without a fight."

With a cigarette hanging from the side of her mouth, Raven walked past the others and retraced her steps back down the corridor. Her heels whispered off the hard floor and she didn't even look at the green room as she went by, approaching the upper staircase.

She descended each step without hurrying, stopping on the landing.

She stared at the door.

"When they come in," Raven said, pointing the Glock downstairs towards the entrance, "I'm going to take out as many as I can before they turn me into a smoothie. The last thing anyone can take away from you is your attitude in any set of given circumstances. Somebody famous said that once."

Dani and Em followed her to the landing. Without saying a word, Dani snatched the Glock out of Raven's hands.

Raven took the Marlboro out of her mouth, stamping it out on the floor. "What the fuck Dani?"

"I say we go back to the green room," Dani said.

There was a nervous reluctance written all over Raven's face. She glanced up at the second floor. "Go back up there? With two grinners inside?"

"Yeah."

Dani wanted it badly. The confrontation. As well as having unfinished business in the green room, she felt a strange sensation growing inside her. It was like feeling drunk but better. Much better. It was almost transcendent. The shit had well and truly hit the fan but Dani had never felt more in control of her life than she did at that moment. The ship was sinking, but that was okay.

She felt a twitch in her right arm. The bitch was still there, still trying to get her attention. Still playing mind games.

"We need a place to hide," Dani said. "Because if those grinners at the front door get in and find us standing here, we're screwed. This isn't the time for last stands Raven, at least not yet. We can live through this but we gotta take the green room back from Creed and the electrician. Then we can lay low, lock the door and wait till the grinners lose interest. After that, we can secure this place properly."

"Yeah but why the green room?" Raven asked. "There's gotta be somewhere else to hide. Somewhere without grinners. Without…"

Dani nodded. "A dead body, I know. But you know better than I do Raven, that it's the best place to hold up. It's got space, a bathroom, food and drink to keep us going for a while. And besides, if we get cornered by those things we can always jump out the window."

"Jump?" Em said. "From the second floor?"

"I'm talking about jumping head first," Dani said. "If it comes to that."

Em was about to respond when a set of plodding footsteps at the top of the stairs cut her off.

Darryl staggered downstairs towards the three women. When he reached the landing, he leaned his body up against the wall, no longer singing but moaning softly like someone nursing a bad hangover.

"Why does he keep following us?" Em asked.

Dani stared at her husband. By now he looked like a torn shroud with legs. Everything, including his face, was buried underneath either hanging skin or the white cocoon exterior that was rising towards the surface. About a quarter of Darryl's mouth remained visible. With his nose buried under all that skin, Dani wondered how he could even breathe. It was a chilling reminder that this was the fate that awaited her. Unless she caught a break and turned into one of the Clean.

"Still here?" she asked in a cold voice.

Dani, with the Glock in hand, marched past Darryl, climbing the stairs back to the second floor. "Who's with me?"

Raven caught up with Dani. "You sure about this?"

"We need the green room," Dani said.

Em joined them on the stairs and the three women returned to the second floor. Dani stood outside the green room door, listening to the sound that escaped through the broken panels. Scraping noises. Loud and wet chewing. Slurping.

She winced. "Oh Christ."

Her body shook. Felt like there was ice water flowing in her veins.

"Okay," she whispered. "Okay, we're doing this."

She walked towards the door. Dani took a deep breath, then stood on her tiptoes as she peered through the gap.

She swallowed the urge to scream.

Creed and the electrician were still on their knees beside Chiara. Dani's sister was flat on her back, arms and legs outstretched to form a star shape. The grinners had punched a deep hole in her chest, allowing room for the methodical excavation that had followed.

Dani watched, hypnotized as they ate the last of Chiara's heart. She resisted the urge to run, to puke, to end up as a sniveling wreck, pounding the floor with both hands and with snot and tears running all over her face. She *would* grieve, but not now.

"Dani," Em whispered. "What's happening?"

Dani felt the last of the dizziness pass. She backed away from the door, shaking her head.

"You don't want to know."

She looked at the Glock in her hands. Guns, she hated guns. Not because they were violent or because of all the stuff on the news, but because they reminded Dani those weekends at the shooting range on West 21st Street with Darryl. Shooting was one of Darryl's favorite things. One of *Darryl's* favorite things, and those were the sort of things they did as a couple. Dani always wondered if Darryl had loved shooting quite as much however, after she'd come off the sidelines and partaken in a little target practice herself. And when she'd turned out to be a better shot than he was? How did that feel? Christ, that must have pissed him off.

Small victories and all.

Nonetheless, Dani thought, shooting at paper targets was one thing.

"We're going in," she said.

She felt a hand on her shoulder. It was a strong hand, holding her in place.

"He's my little brother."

Dani brushed Em's hand away and kept her eyes on the door. "Your little brother is eating my sister's heart in there. Fuck him. Get your mind right Em."

12

The electrician stood to attention as Dani led the charge back into the green room to reclaim the stolen territory. The blond grinner stretched to its full height, letting the meaty pieces in its hands trickle through the gaps in its fingers.

"*muneeeeee, allyoorrwawwwnt.*"

Creed was a little slower to react to the intrusion. But he did, straightening up whilst chewing monotonously on the elder Pellerino's heart. The lower half of his face was soaked in red.

"You bastards," Dani hissed.

"Shoot them Dani," Raven said.

The electrician sprang forward, limbs dangling loose and wild. It was a bizarre, inefficient maneuver, like someone still learning how to operate the human body taking it for a test drive. Nonetheless, it was fast.

Dani extended her reach, pointing the Glock at the electrician. As she focused her aim, the rest of the world slowed down and blurred at the edges. From somewhere afar, she heard a high-pitched siren wailing its way through the night.

Her finger caressed the trigger but nothing happened when her brain sent the command to follow through. She couldn't squeeze. Her trigger finger was paralyzed.

"Dani!" Raven screamed.

The electrician was in front of her. He grabbed Dani's outstretched arms and the sensation of those grasping fingers on her skin was enough to disrupt her brain freeze. There was a noise in her head, an explosion of shattering glass.

Dani yanked her arms free of the grinner's clumsy grip. Her feet moved ahead of her brain and she took a solitary step backwards, opening up a little room in between them again. With her arms held out, rigid and steady, she squeezed the trigger. There was a loud crack. It sounded like a cannon going off inside the green room. The bullet hit the electrician square in the chest, throwing him backwards several paces until he slammed into the edge of the pool table.

The grinner remained on its feet, head tilted to one side, as if processing the sensation of being shot. Then it charged at Dani again, moving like some twitchy, awkward character on an ancient piece of black and white film.

Blood poured from the gunshot wound on its chest. That wasn't enough to stop it or even slow it down. Its long arms yearned for the three women, blood-soaked finger-nails biting at the air in anticipation of a fresh catch.

Dani was on the retreat. As she moved towards the door, the pistol's grip was slippery.

"C'mon!" she screamed, trying to rouse herself back onto the front foot.

She stopped moving backwards. Then she fired again. The muzzle tilted upwards, sending the bullet straight through the grinner's chest again. It didn't go down.

"Fucking die already," Raven said, sounding increasingly desperate.

The electrician stood in front of the women, poking his index finger into the second hole in his chest. It explored the surface-level at first and then it went deeper, probing and jabbing into the flesh as if trying to locate a lost quarter. There was a strange, childlike curiosity in its actions.

"*lurvyooorrr.*"

Dani's heart was thumping. She stepped forward, firing one, two, three rounds, peppering the electrician's midsection and sending it back across the room. Its legs buckled. Finally it toppled over, its head clattering off the steel corner plates of the pool table on the way down.

The electrician rolled back and forth on the carpet, legs kicking like an insect that couldn't get back to its feet. The chest went up and down, fast at first and eventually slowing to a stop. The milky white eyes rolled over several times, and to the surprise of Dani, a set of pale blue eyes filled the emptiness.

Em gasped. "Did you see that?"

Dani saw it. For the first time, she was looking at the electrician. Martin or Mark or Marty or whatever his name had been. There he was, right at the very end.

Creed, who'd watched events unfold from afar while eating, now trampled over its fallen comrade. He raced towards the women. The stiff jaw, no longer chewing, called to them in that raspy voice that ached with longing.

"*lurvyooorr, muneeee.*"

Dani stood her ground, tracking Creed's movement with the Glock. She realized, at the worst possible moment, that she didn't know how many bullets were left in the magazine. *If* there were any left at all. She'd used up what? At least four or five putting the electrician away?

Only one way to find out.

Her finger caressed the trigger. She saw the grin. That fucking evil grin, painted in Chiara's blood.

"Fuck you."

She was about to squeeze when a hand grabbed her bicep and tugged viciously on her arm, knocking Dani off balance. That perfect shot she'd lined up was ruined.

"What the hell?"

Before she could even turn around, Dani felt a powerful arm hooking itself around her waist. Tight. Someone was dragging her towards the door and doing so at a tremendous speed. Taking her out of the green room, back towards the corridor.

Raven's voice was shrill and confused. "Em! Stop it! Stop it now for God's sake."

Dani glanced over her shoulder and saw that Em, in a feat of remarkable strength, was steering both Dani and Raven to the door simultaneously. She had an arm hooked around Dani's waist while she was shoving Raven backwards, using her body as a giant swatter to control Raven's movement, ensuring that the bartender only went where Em wanted her to go. The Academy owner's face was twisted in fierce concentration.

"He's still in there," Em said, her voice shaking uncontrollably. "Creed's still in there, still my brother, and you ain't killing him."

They were back in the dimly lit corridor. Em unhooked her arm from around Dani's waist, hurried back to the door and slammed it shut. Creed, only seconds behind them, walked face first into the door. He immediately started slapping the interior with both hands and to Dani's horror, the beat was in perfect time with the grinners pounding on the front door.

Dani looked at the handle. She knew the door wasn't locked and that if the grinner wanted to open it the quick, easy and old-fashioned way, all it had to do was tap into the host's memory. But the grinner's excitement for the hunt was up and with any luck, that excitement was a distraction, taking it away from thoughts of the host's memory. But for how long? And besides, Dani knew that the grinner was capable of opening a door with brute force if it really wanted to. Either way, Creed wouldn't be in there for long.

What the fuck had Em done?

"Stay there," Em said, talking to her brother in a gentle voice. She almost slipped her hand through the gap in the panels, trying to touch his face. But she stopped and pulled her arm away. "Stay there, just for now until we get a handle on this. I love you and you have to trust me. Okay?"

Creed grinned as he sluggishly pounded on the door. *"lurrvyooorr."*

Dani's heartbeat was so intense that it felt like it was going to explode inside her. She ran at Em, dragging her away from the door. She pointed the gun at her, stabbing the air with the barrel as she spat out the words.

"What the fuck are you thinking you crazy bitch? I almost had him. I almost did it!"

"He's my brother!" Em screamed, shoving Dani backwards. Tears streamed down her cheeks. "And now we know for sure – he's still in there. You saw the electrician's eyes. There's no doubt about that now – they're still in there, still in those bodies."

Dani lowered the Glock. There was a throbbing pain in her head; it felt like someone taking a hammer to her skull. It wasn't helped by the ceaseless banging on the front door or by Creed's lethargic beat coming from the green room.

"I can get him back," Em said, trying to sound calm. "We gotta keep him in there, away from everything until..."

"I'm going to fucking blow his head off," Dani yelled. "And you better start dealing with it Em because we need the green room. Us. We need it before those things at the door get in and start ripping our hearts out."

Creed hit the door harder. *Bang, bang, bang!*

Em backed off towards her brother, shaking her head. "You ain't killing my brother. You want him, you're going to have to go through me first. Because, now that I know he's still in there, I'll fight to the death for him. He's my blood."

Raven stepped forward. "Em, don't get too..."

Creed's arm shot through the gap. The massive fingers wrapped themselves around Em's neck and he squeezed.

"*muneeee.*"

Em tried to speak but all that came out was a muffled choking noise. Her arms windmilled as she tried to wriggle free of her brother's grip. Her long arm moved behind her to the right. The fingers on her hand flirted with the door handle. She missed and the hand slipped off the brass. She tried again, this time securing position.

Dani understood what Em was trying to do. The best way to relieve the pressure of the choke was to pull the door open, bending Creed's limb towards an impossible angle that would force him to relinquish the hold.

It was a good idea. But it would also leave the door wide open.

"Wait!" Dani said.

Em pulled the door and it creaked open. She tried to lean forward and use her weight to hurry it up, her legs bent at the knees. The door swung towards the corridor and Creed's arm was twisted to the point where he had to let go.

Raven hurried over, offering her hand to Em. "C'mon."

But before she could help Em, Creed appeared in the gap in the doorway. His white eyes were dazzling against his bluish-black skin and when he saw his sister, doubled over and recovering after the near fatal choke, he pounced on her.

"*lurvyoowworr.*"

Dani raised the pistol and tried to get a lock on Creed.

Em, trapped in Creed's arms again, saw what Dani was doing and shook her head. Her voice sounded strangled. "No! Don't do it."

Dani adjusted her aim, gliding the barrel past Em and training it on Creed's head. She squeezed the trigger and heard the impotent click that signaled an empty magazine and chamber.

Dani stared in horror at the Glock.

Raven twitched, like she wanted to run over and help her boss. But something held her back.

Meanwhile, Creed grabbed a hold of Em's long black hair and began pulling her towards the door. Em winced, then let out a high-pitched scream that rivalled anything they'd heard across the city that night.

"Let go!" she yelled. "Creed, it's me. It's Em. Emmmmm!"

She managed to break free of Creed's grip and bounce back to her feet. The two siblings wrestled one another as they backed through the open doorway and returned into the green room. They went down. Their legs and arms were tied up in a clumsy knot of limbs. Eventually, Creed managed to wrap a long, snake-like arm around the back of Em's neck, hooking it in tight and fast. He then fastened his other arm around her legs and jumped back to his feet, cradling his sister.

"*lurvyooor.*"

He began to push both ends together, squeezing Em's

legs towards the neck and vice versa. There was a snapping noise, like a giant stick breaking.

Em screamed and then went silent.

Creed let go, dropping the limp body to the floor. Then he fell to his knees and extended his dagger knuckles in the air.

Dani was holding onto Raven's arm, stopping her from doing anything stupid like trying to intervene in a lost cause. She heard a wet slicing noise as Creed's hand disappeared into the dark flesh, probing, a giant worm moving underneath the surface. He continued his excavation in a methodic, workmanlike manner. He was grinning, but there was no emotion in his eyes.

Raven took the gun off Dani. Even though it was empty, she stood in the doorway, pointing it at Creed and squeezing the trigger over and over. Her vampire cheeks were wet with tears.

"How could you? She loved you."

She threw the Glock at Creed and it sailed past his head.

Dani was still trying to pull Raven away from the green room when there was a loud bang inside the building. Several more of these sudden bangs occurred, each one louder than the last. Sounded like the city falling down. And then, a rush of noise like a stampede, something that could have been a freight train speeding over the Academy's roof.

Dani and Raven exchanged horrified looks. Dani let go of Raven's arm and slowly turned towards the balcony.

"They're in."

LOOP 12 - MIMICRY

Hugh Sharkey, naturalist, national treasure and elder statesman of British wildlife documentaries, sits facing the camera.

Pillar candles and tealights fill the background, casting a bioluminescent glow over a darkened room.

Sharkey, 75, speaks with a soft, whispery voice that's as familiar to the British public as a disappointing summer. His long silver hair hangs loose over his shoulders.

HUGH SHARKEY: Good evening. It's a little past two o'clock in the morning here in the UK as we film this special broadcast for the Loop.

Sharkey throws a worried glance at a nearby window as if something outside has disturbed his train of thought. He looks at the camera, pressing a finger to his lips.

Eventually, after almost a minute of silence, he continues.

HUGH SHARKEY: I want to talk to you about the hatchlings and their behavior. I, along with my wife Jill, who's behind the camera, have witnessed some of this strange behavior around our home here in West Sussex tonight. For now, we're staying in the house and keeping our heads down and hoping like so many of you, that help is on its way. We're fortunate enough to have plenty of supplies and both Jill and I have been officially Clean for about two months now. Our children and grandchildren are all okay too. So despite everything that's happening, we still count our blessings.

JILL SHARKEY: Tell them what you've discovered about the hatchlings.

Sharkey nods.

HUGH SHARKEY: Yes. As you all know, I've been studying the natural world for well over fifty years now. My experience in that field has led me to form something of a crude theory about the hatchlings, based on what we saw earlier this evening. Let's examine their behavior, shall we? First of all, have you noticed what they're saying? It's a little hard to make out but I believe, after making some recordings and studying them for the past two hours, that I've figured it out. Contrary to popular opinion, it's not nonsense. The hatchlings, I believe, are trying to communicate with us.

JILL SHARKEY: Bad language warning.

HUGH SHARKEY: Absolutely. But in these circumstances, one must do what one has to in order to educate. And it's all for the greater good. Okay, here we go. I've marked out four separate words and phrases:

Money. Fuck me. Love you. All you want.

That's all I've heard so far, repeated over and over again. And you may have noticed that these words are always spoken to the prey, never to one another.

JILL SHARKEY: And the smile?

HUGH SHARKEY: Yes, the smile. For me, this is the most unsettling thing of all. So what's going on with all of this? The words, the smile, the cannibalism – it all adds up to one thing in my opinion. And this is where my crude theory comes in. I believe that we're witnessing a type of mimicry. Mimicry exists in nature. Mimics evolve to resemble another species and this is done for several reasons: to avoid predation, to increase mating opportunities and in the case of the hatchlings, to capture prey. Signals are made to manipulate prey behavior.

JILL SHARKEY: It's aggressive mimicry isn't it darling? Just to be specific.

HUGH SHARKEY: Yes. With aggressive mimicry, the predator imitates the behavior or sound of the prey. For example, the margay, a small cat native to Central and South America, imitates the call of the pied tamarin monkey in order to lure it closer. The hatchlings however, are practicing a much cruder version of aggressive mimicry. It's crude because unlike species that have evolved this strategy over a long period of time, the hatchlings are, I believe, using the host brain to guide their behavior. Somehow they've tapped into our memories, identifying things that will tempt us, things that will lure us in, things embedded in our mindset as desirable. Money, love and sex.

JILL SHARKEY: That's the bait.

HUGH SHARKEY: Judging by their vocalizations, yes that's the bait. In nature, animals often use the promise of nourishment as a means of attracting prey. In this case, the hatchlings are promising us pleasure. Now here's the thing, the hatchlings are doing a terrible job of it. This predatory virus, if that's what we're dealing with, has underestimated the extent of human intelligence. No one is falling for the mimicry strategy. No one is falling for the promise of sex or money or love, and we're not fooled by the over-the-top smile either that's supposed to lure us in. But the virus has chosen to test this aggressive mimicry strategy and it's testing it as we speak. That's my theory anyway.

JILL SHARKEY: And yet Hugh, despite the fact that no one is falling for it, people *are* approaching the hatchlings. They think their friends and family are coming back to them. We saw it here tonight with that little girl on the main street running towards her dad. Or what she thought was her dad. People want to believe that it's still their loved ones inside those familiar-looking bodies.

Sharkey runs a hand through his long silver mane.

HUGH SHARKEY: Yes, that's true. And perhaps, because of that, the virus won't need to evolve past the mimicry strategy.

JILL SHARKEY: What do you mean darling?

HUGH SHARKEY: Look around you Jill. A lot of people are dying tonight and the virus will feed well. This success *will* be attributed to the mimicry strategy.

A pause.

JILL SHARKEY: One more question and then we'll upload the video. Okay? What's the end goal?

HUGH SHARKEY: An end goal? For the virus?

JILL SHARKEY: Yes. What does it want?

HUGH SHARKEY: Hmmm, as long as the virus can feed and sustain itself then it'll keep moving throughout the population as it's doing now. What then? Well, if it runs out of people, the virus will either die or move into another species of animal and start all over again. Who knows for sure? We can only speculate on things like end goals. Perhaps the destruction of life is its overall purpose. If this thing came to Earth from a cosmic dust storm, then perhaps it has already destroyed many other worlds. Perhaps it feeds on the population of a particular planet until there's nothing left. And then it moves on and all life on that world is forgotten. Whatever the end goal is darling, it's painful to envision what things will look like when the virus has run its course on Earth.

13

Raven ran out of the green room. She had the Glock in her hand once again.

Dani, not knowing why the bartender had bothered going back for an empty pistol, kicked the door shut, locking Creed in again. Luckily, Creed hadn't paid any attention to Raven as she'd hurried back into the green room. He was down on his knees on the floor, still digging around in search of his sister's heart.

The two women peered over the edge of the balcony. Watching as the grinners invaded the Academy.

"Now we're fucked," Raven said in a hushed voice. "Really fucked."

Up until now, Dani's knowledge of the grinners started and ended with Creed and the electrician. Now she was looking at all sorts of shapes and sizes and types. Looked like a convention of grinners down there on the first floor. Female grinners. Child grinners. Elderly grinners. There were even two crippled grinners, dragging themselves across the floor on their palms, scurrying back and forth so fast it looked like they were practicing for the Paralympics.

The invaders explored the first floor, investigating the bar, poking at the empty bottles lined up on the countertop, kicking down barstools, and studying their reflections in the mirror at the back.

It wasn't long before they saw Darryl. What was left of him.

He was sitting on the lower staircase, about halfway up towards the landing. He was cross-legged, swaying back and forth, half-man, half-blob. Dani looked over at her husband and wondered if he was even aware of the grinner invasion.

Some of them began to approach the stairs. They stared up at Darryl, heads tilted in that dog-like curious manner. None of them spoke and they didn't seem to be in any hurry to catch him.

Dani gently lifted the Glock out of Raven's hand.

"You went back for this," she whispered. "Please tell me there's a good reason for that."

Raven nodded and mouthed the words quietly. "I think there's another box of ammo in the office. One, maybe two if we're lucky."

Dani looked at the pistol and then Raven. "And how would you feel about going up there? About finding out for sure?"

Raven didn't answer. She was staring at the weird faceoff between Darryl and the grinners over at the stairs. Her body was tense, shoulders stiff and inwards-facing, as if they were caving in on the rest of her.

"Raven?"

"Huh?"

"Bullets," Dani said. "We need bullets. Go get them and meet me back here. We still have to take the green room off Creed and do it before those things figure out where the stairs lead to."

Raven nodded. She took the gun and like a toy with fresh batteries, bounced back to her feet and hurried along the corridor towards the stairs leading up to the third floor.

Dani turned her attention back to downstairs. Darryl was still in the same spot, methodically peeling the loose skin on his arms. The grinners were still watching him at the foot of the stairs.

"They know," Dani whispered. "They know you're almost one of them." But was being almost one of them enough to keep the grinners off? Hadn't Larry been an 'almost' before Creed caught up with him in the office?

Dani stared at Darryl, thinking how pitiful he looked. God, he really was pitiful. But somewhere in the wreckage down there was the too good to be true guy she'd met in high school. Handsome, ambitious, popular – blah, blah, blah. Wasn't it always so? The stud athlete and the cute, talented girl who could sing and play guitar better than anyone else in school. Such promising beginnings that led to fifteen years of treading water and occasional bouts of drowning. They'd become a cliché – the popular kids who'd failed at being grown-ups.

But it wasn't all Darryl's fault. Dani had lost herself in inertia and cowardice and that was her fault. She told herself that unhappiness was her lot in life and then used that as an excuse to do nothing about it. This was her reward – the constant burden of failure and the feeling of always being a stranger in her own skin. Damn it. She felt like she was destined for so much more in life and yet whatever that was, it had never revealed itself. Or more likely the case, Dani had missed it. She'd screwed up all by herself. Darryl was little more than a piece of background furniture in a sad story.

The soft pitter-patter of footsteps crept up behind her.

Raven was holding up the Glock. There was an encouraging smile on her face.

"That was quick," Dani said quietly.

"Yeah."

"Any luck?"

"Fully loaded. But that's the last of the ammo."

Dani took the gun and ran her thumb over the grip. "Stay here. I'll be back in a minute."

"Where are you going?"

"Just sit tight and stay here."

"Dani, what the hell?"

Dani walked towards the staircase, bent over at first and then she straightened up, no longer caring if they saw her or not. She walked at a slow, measured pace. After descending the upper staircase, she found herself on the landing, close to where Darryl was sitting halfway down the second set of stairs.

She stared at a sea of grinners looking back at her.

"Get up Darryl," Dani said through gritted teeth. She could feel the Glock shaking in her grip.

"Get up. I want you to stand up and turn around towards me. Okay?"

Darryl was still peeling. He gave no indication that he'd heard her.

One of the grinners, a skinny male with a shaved head, raised his foot onto the staircase. Behind him, Dani could see the others becoming more animated.

"*furkmeeerr.*"

She stood her ground, although her legs were shaking in a way that she'd never experienced before. "Darryl. Get up you fucking idiot. I want you to look at me."

At last, Darryl stopped peeling, releasing a long sheet of papery white skin attached to his right forearm. When he turned around, most of his face was white. His mouth had vanished altogether. He looked like a dark fairy tale monster, something that chased little children in the woods.

"I'm not going to die for you Darryl. If you can understand me, get up and walk upstairs at a steady pace. Your legs still work."

There were more grinners on the stairs. Following the shaven-headed leader who reached for Dani.

"*allyooorwawnt, muneeee.*"

Dani crept downstairs, her insides churning as she walked towards them. She stopped in front of the white lump and kicked its back. She felt how much softer he was already. It was like kicking a slab of marshmallow.

"Darryl!"

Dani thought she could hear muffled laughter inside that almost-cocoon. Or was it crying? Was he mad and screaming as he slipped away?

Nonetheless, Darryl stood up and reached for Dani.

"*lurvvyooo,*" an old woman grinner said. She was about seventy and yet she'd slipped ahead of the pack, grinning so hard that even her wrinkles had wrinkles.

Dani was well aware that they were coming. It felt like she was standing on the edge of a cliff, leaning over a steep drop and ignoring the strong wind at her back. She could hear Raven whisper-shouting from the second floor.

"Dani. Get out of there for God's sake!"

Dani grabbed Darryl and he almost lost his balance. She slapped him hard on the spongy head, trying to bring him back. Trying to bring *Darryl* back before Burn swallowed him up for good. The stink of body odor was lethal, not just from Darryl, but the collective perfume of the grinners on the first floor. It was the same foul and sweet stench she'd smelled in the office after Creed's hatching.

Darryl's one remaining eye blinked hard in between the dead skin. It looked like he was trying to focus on his wife. And there it was. Dani recognized the moment he came back, just by the look in his eye. There was a lifetime of familiarity in that single exchange. He was himself again – Darryl McBride.

"Will you come with me?" she asked. "If I get you out of here?"

Nothing. Darryl just blinked.

"Just nod if you can hear me Darryl. Do you want to come with me? I need to know for sure that it's still you."

A faint nod of the head.

Dani smiled at him. "Thanks Darryl. I'm glad it's still you in there. Because if I know it, I'll bet you anything they know it too."

She spun him around on the step. Now he was facing the grinner pack on the stairs. Dani grabbed the back of his head, twisting it left and right, letting them see, letting the grinners see his one good eye. Now that he was back, would they see it? Would they see a man just like Creed had seen a man in Larry?

She heard him. Now he was definitely screaming through the cocoon mask. It was faint, like someone screaming from two blocks away. But there it was.

Dani leaned towards the closed-up space where Darryl's ear was supposed to be. "Did you really think I came down here to save you? *You?* You killed Chiara."

The muffled screaming continued. Darryl tried to turn around and face Dani, but there was no time and his movement was slow, weighed down by the burden of transformation that was pressing down on him. Dani lashed out, kicking Darryl in the back. One was all it took. He rolled downstairs like a boulder into the arms of the waiting grinners. Just the movement was enough to trigger them. They reached for Darryl. They grabbed him before he could reach the bottom and fought over him. Those in control pulled Darryl down to the floor where there was more room to work. Others followed the leaders back downstairs, still fighting to gain possession of the prize.

The excitement. Their cries, it was deafening.

Dani couldn't even begin to count the number of hands stabbing into the flesh. She had no intention of trying either.

There were a few grinners on the stairs, their focus still firmly on Dani. She aimed the Glock at the ones nearest to her, firing repeatedly, watching as the grinners fell backwards like paper targets at a funfair. They cracked their heads open on the stairs on the way down. It was a delicious sound and Dani could have stood there all day listening to it.

She didn't realize that the gun was empty. Not until she felt Raven tugging on her arm, leading her back towards the stairs.

"C'mon!" Raven said.

They went back to the second floor. The rotten body odor lingered in Dani's nostrils as she let the Glock slip through her fingers.

"Fucking hell," Raven said, gasping for breath. "Dani, you killed him. Is...is that why you went down there? To wipe him out like that?"

"He killed Chiara," Dani said. "And I don't care if you believe me or not."

"Hey," Raven said, hands up in the air. "It's none of my business what divorce looks like nowadays. But what do we do now?"

Dani pointed at the green room. "Now we take it back

once and for all. It's a simple choice. Either we take our chances with one grinner in there or with a hundred out here. What do you say Raven?"

Raven wiped at a smudge of thinning makeup on her neck. Her natural skin tone, darker than Dani had expected it to be, was starting to seep through.

"What do I think?" Raven said. "I think nothing's changed Dani. But all things considered, I'll take my chances against Creed."

THE LOOP IS DOWN

Please be patient while we fix critical errors.

14

Creed was on his knees, doubled over in between the two dead women when Dani and Raven came back to take the green room.

Em and Chiara didn't look like people anymore. They were sprawled out side by side on the blood-soaked carpet. Their arms and legs were broken, the limbs pointing in impossible directions. They looked like horror movie props; mannequins that had been tortured by a pack of sadistic schoolchildren.

Dani had to put aside all the emotion that would distract her from the task at hand. She closed the door quietly behind her.

Creed's white eyes shone as he saw the two women entering the room. He had Em's heart in his hands and he was still chewing on the cone-shaped organ, his jaw grinding down the meat with a dull, lethargic rhythm.

He stood up. Dani thought she heard his joints cracking.

"*furkmeeerr, allyooorwawwwnt.*"

Raven jumped over the dead electrician and ran to the edge of the pool table. Keeping her eyes on Creed, she grabbed both cues and slid them off the baize. Then she carried them back to the door.

She tossed a cue to Dani. "Ready?"

"Ready," Dani said, catching the stick and securing an immediate grip around the butt.

Creed's head tilted to the side. He dropped Em's heart, not that there was much left, at his bare feet.

"*muneeee, muneeee.*"

He plodded across the room towards them. Dani and Raven exchanged a brief glance, then lashed out, thrusting their cue shafts forward like spears. This strategy allowed them to keep Creed at a distance, as long as he couldn't get past the cues.

Dani stabbed the tip at his head, searching for a clean shot at Creed's eyes. She hit a lot of air and poked the left cheek once, but apart from pushing Creed back a little, that one successful blow had little if any affect.

Raven switched tactics. Gripping the top end tight with both hands, she tried to club Creed over the head with the thicker, more solid butt end. She made a hard karate style noise with each strike. But it was no use. Fighting off Creed with a pool cue was like trying to blow back a category five hurricane. He was already pushing both women onto the backfoot, forcing them back to the door.

Dani kept spearing at the grinner's eyes, stabbing over and over again. She was relentless, knowing that she couldn't pause and give him any time to launch a counter attack. But try as she might, Dani couldn't get close enough to land a significant hit, at least not while keeping a safe distance.

"You're not Creed!" Raven hissed.

Both women thrust and jabbed, trying to retain their balance on the bloody, slippery carpet. There were also three dead bodies on the floor, gruesome booby traps waiting to derail their plans. The green room, Dani thought, felt more like an assault course with a horror movie twist than it did a place for bands to hang out before and after gigs.

Creed swatted their flimsy offence away.

"We're getting our asses kicked!" Raven said. "What do we do?"

"Harder!" Dani screamed, stabbing over and over again, too frightened to call off the attack in case she noticed the fatigue. "The eyes. Aim for the eyes!"

"I'm trying. He's too far back."

She was right. They had to get closer. And although it was in all likelihood certain death, it was their only chance of landing anything significant. The knockout blow. Something that might stop Creed in his tracks and give them an opportunity to pile the match-winning hurt on. They just needed one good shot to start things off.

Dani knew she had to set an example.

She leaped forward, screaming and tilting the cue upwards at Creed's face. After about ten straight misses, she felt the tip land in the soft flesh of Creed's left eye. Electricity soared through her body. She felt like she'd just made the winning kick in the Superbowl.

But the blow didn't derail Creed. Despite the redness that gathered around the damaged eye, he kept coming, arms fully extended in the direction of Dani and Raven.

"*lurvvyooowwr.*"

Raven dropped her pool cue onto the carpet. "This is hopeless."

"Keep going," Dani called out, wanting to sound encouraging and enraged at the same time. "Don't quit."

"Dani," Raven said. "We can't win."

Dani didn't take her eyes off Creed for a second. She could feel her body filling up with the weight of exhaustion. "We just hurt him."

"Dani, c'mon! Look at him for God's sake. He's still coming."

"No."

As if to underline the fact that she was going nowhere, Dani launched her most ferocious attack yet, which bordered on the downright kamikaze in terms of recklessness. She came within the danger zone and stabbed the butt end of the cue at the grinner's midsection, doing so with such brute force that Creed, who was at least sixty pounds heavier than Dani, was pushed back.

The grinner's head tilted to the side.

Dani spat in Creed's direction. Despite her love of all things old school punk, she'd never spat at anyone in her life.

"C'mon," she said. "C'mon."

She barely acknowledged the disruptive force behind her.

"I'm not going to die here Dani," Raven said, tugging on Dani's right shoulder. "My arms are like lead. Look, it didn't work out. Let's go!"

"There's nowhere else to go," Dani said, keeping her eyes on Creed. She barely recognized her own voice and realized it was because she sounded like Chiara. "This is our room. We can't fail."

Raven stared at the bodies on the floor. "Dani, I'm scared. I'm shit scared, okay? Let's just go and conjure up a Plan B and we'll..."

"No! Go if you want and close the door behind you."

Dani wriggled free of the bartender's grip. Raven's hand slipped off Dani's shoulder and she looked so shocked that

Dani might as well have slapped her on the face. Her eyes were hollow. Defeated.

"You'll die if you stay here."

"Go."

"Dani, please. We have to stick together if we're going to make it through this. We've lost the green room for God's sake but there's..."

"Go!"

Creed was coming forward again, far from discouraged by Dani's one good shot to the eye. He brought all his hunger and longing with him, as well as that foul stink of body odor. Meanwhile Raven's footsteps receded towards the door. There was a creaking noise as it swung open and then, although Raven closed the door quietly, it sounded like a clap of thunder in Dani's head.

And yet for some reason that she couldn't understand, at least not then, she welcomed it. It was like being locked in a room with certain death. And she wasn't afraid. On the contrary, she was inspired.

Nonetheless, the pool stick wasn't up to the job. It was like fighting a silverback gorilla with a pencil.

But what choice did she have?

Dani wiped the sweat off her brow. "C'mon Creed."

Creed lunged at her. Dani saw it coming and side-stepped the attack with ease, spearing the grinner in the ribs as he came in. Nice hit. She felt focused. Ready to use her legs a little more and give her arms some much needed respite.

Dani spun around in a clockwise direction, keeping to the outskirts of room. Creed followed and she slipped just out of range whenever Creed tried to grab a hold of her. He seemed confused by these evasive maneuvers. He was off balance whenever he missed a grab. Dani had to leap over

Chiara and Em on the floor on several occasions, just to keep out of reach of Creed's long arms. Creed showed no such respect for the dead, trampling over the bodies, over their heads, as he chased Dani around the room.

She climbed up onto the pool table, digging her heels into the baize. At least it wasn't slippery up there.

"C'mon Creed."

From up high, she speared downwards as if fighting off invaders trying to scale the castle wall.

"Bastard!"

But Creed, in true grinner fashion, kept coming. He put both hands on the pool table, seemingly on the brink of joining Dani up there. Dani had no intention of confining this game of cat and mouse to an area with dimensions of no more than a hundred inches by fifty. As Creed climbed onto the pool table and made a hissing noise at her, Dani jumped off.

She gasped for breath after the hasty landing. Her muscles filled with lactic acid, which made the pool cue feel like it had twenty kilo weights dangling off both ends.

There was a hard thud as Creed jumped off the pool table.

"*allyooorrwaawwwnt.*"

Dani spun around. Now the grinner was in front of the door, blocking off her exit should she change her mind.

She glanced at the window, then turned back to Creed. Fuck it, she wasn't ready to jump either. Then, as her eyes scoured the room in search of inspiration or a gamechanger, she found both. It was a crumpled black object on the red couch. Her backpack. The zip was pulled open about halfway across the track, revealing the tip of something that made Dani's heart sing.

Dani Machete's machete handle.

"*muneee, allyooorwawnt.*"

Creed scurried forward, fingers snapping. His grin stretched to breaking point. Dani threw the pool cue across the room like a javelin and it sailed past the grinner's head, hitting the door. That moment was all she needed.

Dani pounced to her left, her lead foot sliding on something she didn't want to know about. She hurdled over the table, pumping her arms and legs as she zeroed in on the couch. Grabbing the backpack off the cushion, she fought with the zip handle, trying to open up enough space to slide the machete out easily.

The zip was stuck.

"FUCK!" Dani screamed, the metal of the zip biting into the flesh of her fingers.

Loud, crashing footsteps behind her.

"*furkmeeeerr.*"

Dani thrust her fingers into the gap, grabbed both sides of the bag and pulled. Fuck it, after everything she'd survived so far she wasn't going to be outwitted by goddamn backpack. There was a crude, tearing noise that opened up the gap an extra inch or two. Dani shoved her hand inside, clamping her fingers around the rubber handle. She pulled upwards, trying to free the curved blade from the confines of the backpack and whatever other obstacles blocked its route – clothes, accessories and a spare guitar tuner. She felt the machete shift. Then it was stuck. Then it moved again.

"*lurvyooor!*"

"C'MON!"

Dani pulled the weapon through the opening. She spun around, just as Creed was climbing over the table, barely a couple of meters away, all set to pounce. He reached for Dani's heart like a hungry chimpanzee begging for food.

Dani's sweaty fingers secured a tight grip on the hilt. She

took the fight to Creed, slashing wildly and using the serrated edge to cut into Creed's side. A deep, zigzag-shaped gash opened at the waist. Dani jerked the blade up and down while it was still attached to the flesh. More blood spilled from the grinner's waist.

Creed spat out a harsh, exhaling noise. His body spasmed. Dani pulled the machete out and carved open a fresh wound on the grinner's neck, attacking the jugular with the same vicious enthusiasm she'd shown with the pool cue.

Creed's face was a blank. Blood poured from his wounds, spilling onto the carpet.

"*lurvyooor.*"

The words were hollow, stripped of desire.

He fell onto his back, landing close to his sister.

Dani stood back, her clothes covered in blood spray. She was exhausted and exhilarated at the same time. Alive, she felt alive.

She watched as the white orbs rolled over in the grinner's head. Gone, back, then gone again. Seconds later, the dark brown of Creed's eyes appeared in the vacant space. Dani felt like she was looking at the man for the first time. She felt almost ashamed at what she'd done to him.

Almost.

The last thing Creed saw was his sister lying beside him. He tried to speak to her, tried to reach for her, but it was too late.

Dani sat on the floor, staring at the gaping hole in Chiara's chest.

Her sister was lying underneath a dark, oily puddle of blood. Her graying, waxy skin was lifeless. Dani had tried to close Chiara's eyes but they wouldn't stay shut, even though she wasn't long dead and Dani had read somewhere that it was easier to close the eyes of the recently deceased compared to the eyes of those who'd been dead for hours and were in the grip of rigor mortis. But they wouldn't close. They were slightly open, gazing at the ceiling as if waiting for something to happen up there.

Chiara, Em, Creed, the electrician. The floor was littered with corpses.

Dani inhaled a putrid combination of stale cigarette smoke, along with something that smelled like a cocktail of garbage and rotten eggs. Whatever it was, it was enough to trigger the gag reflex at the back of her throat. She jumped to her feet, dropped the machete and ran into the bathroom. Once inside, she fell onto her knees, grabbed a hold of both ends of the toilet and threw up.

"Oh Jesus," she said, bringing her head back up for air.

She pressed her back up against the tiled wall. In the distance, she could hear the grinners' clumsy footsteps and signature raspy mumbles.

"Shit," Dani said, wondering if the hatchling mob was upstairs yet. It just occurred to her that the door, while closed over, wasn't locked.

She hurried back into the green room and found the key lying on the floor, mercifully apart from the bodies. Dani picked it up and slid it back into the lock. The snap of the bolt sliding into place was heaven. But the panels, she had to do something about the broken panels. They were like two windows offering a perfect view of the green room interior.

Dani went down on her knees and crawled over to the nearest wall that was covered in promotional posters. The posters there featured an eclectic mix of bands who'd played at the Academy over the years. She reached up and peeled off one of the bigger ones, an A3-sized flyer advertising a band called Rock Noise Cult, who'd played at the Academy three years ago, March 17th according to the poster. Dani put the flyer in her teeth and crawled back to the door. Quietly, she stood up, listening for any new sounds outside in the corridor. There was nothing, not yet. Working fast, she turned the poster on its side and placed it over the vacant panels, attaching it to the wooden edges with the Scotch tape still hanging off sides. It was a good fit, but the tape was old and a temporary fix that wouldn't last long.

She stepped back from the door, hearing footsteps on the upper staircase. Yeah, they were coming up, some of them at least. And when the rest of them had finished picking up the scraps around Darryl they'd be up too.

Dani closed her eyes and wiped the sweat off her face.

She knew she couldn't hide in the green room forever. Not alone, not like this. Not with the bodies, not with Chiara lying there like that with her eyes still open, looking all broken and dead and yet somehow still alive. There weren't even any sheets or covers, nothing that she could use to put over them.

Was she really ready to put a sheet over Chiara?

She sat down on the battered red couch. Leaning her head against the wall, Dani felt a sudden twitch in her wrist. There was also a tingling sensation beneath the shoulder and it ran down the length of her arm like a slow tease. Dani's fingertips flinched like they'd received a shock.

She felt it. An overwhelming urge to search for dead skin. That was the best way to cool down, wasn't it?

"Oh Christ, leave me alone."

Twitch.

"Here she comes," Dani said, her eyes landing on the body of her sister. "The bitch is back."

Twitch.

Dani's arm shuddered, forcing her to use her good hand to steady the rogue limb. Christ, it was hot. How long could she go on like this? It felt like there was a civil war raging inside her body with the result still unknown.

"Darryl's dead," she said in a quiet voice. "You'll be pleased to hear that. Won't you?"

She tapped a finger off the side of her head.

"Fucker still lives in here though. Can't kill *that* Darryl so easily, more's the pity."

Too restless and fidgety to sit down, Dani jumped back to her feet, listening to the footsteps in the corridor. She wondered if Raven was alright. There were no grudges, at least not as far as Dani was concerned. She didn't have many friends left to lose.

She returned to the bathroom and threw cold water over her face. She drank from the faucet too, not realizing how thirsty she was until she started chucking it down. It didn't taste great, a little metallic maybe, but it was better than nothing. After turning the water off, Dani looked at her reflection in the mirror. Her makeup was fading everywhere. There was a cluster of loose skin visible on her neck, but that was about it as far as she could tell. Her skin wasn't too soft either, which was good. All things considered, Dani wasn't ready to give up on her dream of turning Clean.

She leaned closer to the mirror. Her right arm twitched sporadically.

"Get the hell out of here," Dani said, staring deep into her eyes and wondering if there was something else in there looking back at her.

She stared at her reflection for a long time, waiting for something inside her head to reveal itself. The tired features reflected back at Dani were both familiar and alien. The image blurred, came back into focus, blurred again and then it was rinse and repeat. Who was it looking back at her? Singer? Wife? Survivor? None of those things or all of them? Dani pulled at the skin under the whites of her eyes. Thank God, the brown irises were still rich in color, absent of the fading that was another surefire sign you were on the road to Cocoonsville.

Dani felt her arm twitch again.

She put her head against the cracked glass and glared at her own face up close. "I'm going to beat you."

Her right forearm spasmed, as if responding to Dani's challenge.

Dani slammed her palm against the mirror, almost knocking it off the wall. "You think I'm going to let you steal my body? *My* body. Do you think I'm just going to stand back and let you take my entire life away from me? Okay, okay bitch. I've had enough of this waiting around shit. How about we finish this right here, right now?"

She stormed back into the green room and grabbed the machete off the floor. Returning to the bathroom, she glared at her reflection.

"Time to see what you're made of."

Dani rolled her sleeve all the way up to her right shoulder. Then she placed her Judas arm on the edge of the sink, underside facing up. Still glaring at her reflection, she pushed the serrated edge of the machete against her exposed bicep.

"It's my body," she said. "And if I want to hack an arm off, I'll hack it off. I'll cut off every last piece of flesh you haunt even if it means my life."

Dani tightened her grip on the rubber hilt, waiting for the bitch to react. The next twitch would be the clincher.

"One way or another, I'll shut you up I swear to God."

She pushed the blade down, allowing the teeth to pinch at her skin. It felt like her arm was trapped in the mouth of a mako shark.

"What the fuck are you doing Dani?" a voice said from inside the bathroom.

Dani almost had a heart attack. "What the...?"

"Cut off your arm and you'll never play the guitar again. You realize that, don't you?"

"Chiara?"

It *was* Chiara's voice, drifting in from the green room and resonating around the echo chamber that was the bathroom. Alive, very much alive.

"Don't you ever want to play guitar again?"

Dani's eyes roamed the bathroom, searching for a face in the tiles or a shadowy figure standing in the shower.

The machete remained tight against her arm.

"Chiara? Is that really you?"

"Yeah."

"It's not you. It can't be you."

"Didn't I always shoot straight from the hip Dani? Didn't I though? Take Darryl for instance – everyone loved him when we were kids. Remember? Teachers, parents, the other kids, and you most of all much to my disgust. Not me though, I knew an asshole when I saw one and I saw one from the start when I looked at that asshole. And didn't I let everyone know? And wasn't I right in the end? Always been a truth-teller and to hell with the rest, that's me. I think you're crazy if you let someone else take another piece of you."

"*This* has to stop," Dani said, pressing the blade down slowly. She winced as the skin reddened, then pierced, bringing forth a thin stream of blood that trickled onto the edge of the porcelain.

"You're not thinking about the gig."

"What fucking gig?" Dani said, relieving the pressure and looking around for Chiara's face again. "The show's off. You were there, remember?"

"Dani Machete lives," Chiara said. "Look what you just did to Creed in that room back there. You killed the electrician. And then Darryl, for me. That was Dani Machete, the real deal, grinner killer extraordinaire. Maybe it was never about the guitar for you Dani. Maybe it's in this nightmare, this bizarre fuck-off nightmare, that you'll find your true self. Find out what you can do in the world."

"I don't know what you're talking about Chiara."

Silence.

"Chiara?"

Dani looked up towards the ceiling, half-expecting

Chiara's dead face to be looking down at her, the eyes still open, the mouth frozen in an eternal O-shape.

Dani lifted the machete off her arm and looked in the mirror again. She waited for the twitching to start but it didn't come.

"Dani Machete," she said.

She walked back into the green room and took her stage clothes out of the backpack. As she removed the bloody garments she had on, Dani listened to the grinners outside in the corridor.

"See ya soon," she whispered.

Quickly, she pulled Dani Machete's slashed black and silver t-shirt over her head. The tight-fitting t-shirt sported a pair of faded out, black and white breasts on the front that fit nicely over Dani's real breasts. She sat down on the couch, pulling on a set of skinny black jeans, then slipped her feet into a pair of matching-colored boots with cube heels.

Dani returned to the bathroom, swinging the backpack by the top strap like it was a toy. She resumed her position in front of the mirror.

"Dare you," she whispered. "Try something now."

She pulled out a tub of gel and went to work on her thick, jet-black hair, styling it in honor of one of her punk rock idols, Ari Up from The Slits. The straight out of bed look. Bird's nest hair. After topping up her makeup, Dani took off her glasses, pulled out her contacts and solution, and went to work, holding her eyelids open and placing the lenses in her eyes.

She wiped the dust off the mirror.

"I remember you."

With a smile, she picked up the machete off the floor. It was time to go to work.

16

Dani peeled back the corner of the poster she'd placed over the door. Just a few inches. Just enough to see what was going on out there.

There were about ten grinners on the second floor, circling the balcony area. These grinners represented the beginning of a slow migration from the first floor to the upper levels of the Academy, a migration that would speed up once the excitement over Darryl's body came to an end.

Dani stared at the sad, lumbering shapes out there in the corridor. In between the chase, the grinners' existence was sedate; it was as if they were replenishing their energy supplies in between hunts. Those bodies were still human, weren't they? Still prone to fatigue? Dani wondered what was going on inside their heads. What was driving them? Were they using the host's memories to guide their hunting strategy? Were the grinners, tapping into old habits, visiting old haunts from their previous life? Dani realized that those shapes in the corridor might be some old Academy gig-goers, live music fans going back to what they'd known before? Was that it? Were banker grinners standing outside banks, waiting for the doors to open on Monday morning? Were teacher grinners going back to schools to look for their pupils?

Dani squeezed the rubber hilt of the machete. It felt hot, almost scalding in her grip.

She pulled the door open, thankful that it didn't creak. Her heart was racing. Her throat felt like water hadn't touched it in weeks. As she stepped into the dark corridor, ceiling lights flickering above her head, Dani imagined that she was stepping onto the stage, soaking up the roar of the crowd.

The grinners' bodies twitched when they saw her emerge into the corridor. Their postures stiffened. The white eyes, dull in the absence of the chase, lit up again.

"*furkmeeeerrr.*"

"*lurvyoooooowwrrr.*"

"*allyoooorrrwawwnt.*"

A middle-aged woman was the first to reach Dani. Like all the grinners, she was stark naked and Dani noticed a horizontal scar on the chest where the woman's left breast had been removed. Her face was swollen and purplish-blue. The long fingers snapped like scissors as they reached for Dani's heart.

Dani swung the machete like it was a baseball bat, positioning it over her right shoulder and following through with all her body. She swung for the fences. The blade raked the left side of the woman's face, drawing an immediate, fast-flowing stream of blood. Dani threw her leg out, push-kicking the grinner on the chest. The grinner staggered backwards, slamming into the chrome railing and almost tipping over the edge.

Dani launched a follow up attack, narrowly missing the

grinner's exposed neck. She tried again and the second blow cut so deep that the blade was stuck in the flesh.

"Shit."

Dani felt a surge of panic as she tried to get the machete out. She pulled, forcing the woman's head to jerk wildly back and forth. Meanwhile the excited pitter-patter of footsteps was closing in on all sides as the rest of the grinners caught up with the action.

Blood gushed from the woman's neck, but she was still grinning. Still staring at Dani.

"*furkmeeeerr.*"

Dani pulled the handle down an inch. She carved frantically, slicing deeper into the woman's flesh to open up the wound and release the blade. Droplets of blood sprayed onto her face, Jackson Pollocking her eyes, nose and mouth. It tasted foul, like rot. Dani could only hope that the grinner's blood wasn't infectious.

The machete loosened. With a roar of desperation, Dani pulled it free and staggered backwards.

She spun around, just in time. A huge male grinner was coming at her, its grin exposing a set of yellow, crooked teeth that would have made a dentist faint.

"*allyoorwawwwnt.*"

Dani circled out of danger. Moving wasn't so easy on cube heels as it had been on flats. Also, the floor was slippery with all the blood that had spilled out of the grinner's neck.

There was a fresh platoon of grinners hurrying up the staircase. They must have heard the action from downstairs and now they were on their way, ready to join the fun.

The big male lunged at Dani, trying to close the gap. His hand, with long dirty fingernails, brushed against Dani's shoulder and realizing that he was in close range, she raised the machete handle and slicing in a sudden downwards motion, cut his face open from the bridge of the nose to the chin.

For good measure, she added a kick to the balls. That made the grinner double over and the blood rained down from his facial cut, spilling onto the floor.

Dani slashed in diagonal lines, cutting the man open from top to bottom as if she was transforming him into a modern art exhibition.

He was still on his feet, talking through a mask of blood. "*lurvyooorrr.*"

"Fucking die!" Dani screamed.

A teenage boy grinner charged at her from the right. Dani stepped back and threw a hook-like blow with the machete that sliced open the teenager's head. Her aim was improving, it was definitely improving.

The teenager yelped. It sounded like a small child waking up from a nightmare.

The big male was still on his feet. He looked like someone who'd been attacked by a pack of wolves. He reached out to Dani like a beggar holding up a cup. After a couple of shaky steps, he crashed to the floor, thrashing around like he was drowning on dry land.

Dani saw movement everywhere. She was surrounded by grinners.

And she was getting tired.

She lashed out, swinging the bloody machete from side to side. But there was less brute force and precision in Dani's attack. It was bound to happen. Accuracy would fail her. Strength would fail her. She'd come here to die anyway, hadn't she? To take out as many of the grinners as she could before they got their hands on her.

Dani threw long curving strikes that bought her time.

The grinners' leering faces taunted her. They stared at her with white, starving eyes. Always reaching, reaching for her heart with snapping fingers.

They were in control now. Pushing her around, forcing her to go wherever they wanted her to.

Dani's back brushed up against the railing. She glanced briefly over her shoulder and saw a bloody pile of meat down there on the first floor. Darryl. There was still a large group of grinners gathered around the body, picking at the hole in the chest as if there might be a second heart tucked away somewhere in there.

The grinners on the second floor called to Dani. Wooed her in those raspy, demonic voices.

Exhaustion gave way to fear. But then fear turned into a sudden eruption of anger that swelled up inside Dani. They were taking it away from her. Taking away the dream she'd waited so long to realize and would have realized but for the fucking hatching. All she wanted was the chance to play in front of a live audience, to gauge the reaction and find out, once and for all, if she was any good. It was nothing much and yet, it was everything.

She'd pissed her life away. Just to please everyone else.

Dani was screaming before she even realized she was screaming. It was a wild, throat-killer and it came from somewhere deeper than the heart. Fuck it, why not? She would sing, fuck them all, she *would* sing and die doing something she loved. It's not tragic to die doing something you love, isn't that what Patrick Swayze's character, Bodhi, had said in *Point Break*?

Christ, she was about to get her heart ripped out and she was thinking about *Point Break*.

Dani closed her eyes and jumped into a chorus of 'White Riot' by The Clash. She throttled her larynx, unleashing a primal scream, an articulation of all the hurt she'd stored up inside her over the years.

Her voice was still there.

And she was still there. She was alive.

Dani opened her eyes. The grinners were staring at her. They stood still, their faces uniformly bent out of shape and for the first time, Dani thought, they looked uncomfortable. All grins were receding. Their bodies swayed from side to side, as if their balance had been knocked off-kilter.

Dani's heart skipped a beat. They couldn't take it. Couldn't take the tune.

She caught her breath quickly, then jumped back into another chorus of 'White Riot.' Dani's voice soared and she sang as if she was trying to make herself heard over a fully amplified band.

A cappella warfare.

The grinners' heads twitched like someone who'd experienced the sensation of a fly shooting up their nostrils.

Dani, who was surrounded at the railing, noticed a gap opening up in the sea of bodies in front of her. She began to navigate her way through the escape route, still singing, still letting them have it full blast.

But where now? Now that she'd put a little space between herself and the grinners where was she supposed to go?

Before she could make a decision, Dani saw a hand waving at her from behind the sound desk. The hand went up in the air, beckoned Dani over, then disappeared behind the equipment again. Dani followed the chrome railing in a counterclockwise direction, taking the shortest route to the desk. She only stopped singing 'White Riot' after slipping inside the small, waist high compartment that contained the mixing board.

Raven was sitting on the floor, hugging her knees to her chest. Dani dropped to the floor and they embraced.

"Thank God," Raven said. "You're alright."

Dani nodded. "Are *you* alright?"

Raven shrugged. "I guess. What the fuck was all that about just now?"

Dani pressed a finger to her lips. "Shhhh. I don't think they like my singing."

Raven pointed to Dani's hair and clothes. "Digging the new look by the way."

"Me too," Dani said, trying to catch her breath. She still had a vice-like grip on the machete handle.

"What happened to Creed?"

Dani ran a finger along her throat.

"Wow," Raven whispered, looking at Dani like she was a complete stranger. "You know, I felt like shit running off like that and leaving you alone with him. Really. I was scared, I'm still scared and that's why I'm hiding behind this desk like a total wimp while you're out there kicking ass."

"It's okay," Dani said, peering over the desk at the grinners who were starting to move around again. "I'm shit-scared too, believe me."

Dani looked at the mixing board, a plastic tapestry of faders and buttons and inputs. To the uninitiated it was a spider's web of options.

"Hey," she whispered to Raven. "You were there at the soundcheck, weren't you?"

"For a little while. Why?"

"I'm thinking about the feedback that Larry couldn't quite shake off."

"Happens every time."

Dani pushed herself up to a squatting position, her fingers fiddling with the buttons and faders on the desk. She worked frantically, trying to activate the mic and start a feedback loop inside the Academy. It was a long time since she'd stood in front of a mixing desk, but things hadn't changed that much in fifteen years. Or had they?

"I think the singing disorientated them," Dani whispered. "Imagine what some heavy feedback could do."

Raven got up and tiptoed towards the desk.

"Turn up the gain," she said, gently nudging Dani to the side. "Fader, EQ – fuck it, set everything to stun if you're talking about frying their brains. Lucky for us, some venues are notorious for their feedback. Luckier still, the Academy sits right at the top of that list."

"Yeah I noticed," Dani said.

There was a faint screech from downstairs.

"That's not enough."

"I know but I'm no Larry," Raven said, noticing the disappointment on Dani's face. "Here's the thing Dani – we can create a hell of a lot more noise if someone's down there standing on the stage, putting their hand over the capsule of the mic…"

"Capsule?"

"Just put your hand over the mic. Even better, point the mic at the onstage monitor and this place will be screaming. But listen Dani, cover your ears as best you can 'cos that shit's going to be intense. Long-term damage guaranteed."

Dani looked at the empty stage where her guitar and amp were still waiting. "I'll take a little deafness over having my heart ripped out."

"Fair enough," Raven said. "I got a question."

"What?"

"The feedback stuns them, right?"

"That's what I'm hoping for."

"It stuns them but it doesn't kill them. What's the long-term plan here?"

Dani leaned over the edge of the desk. "The bar's directly underneath us, right? How much of that alcohol down there is flammable?"

Raven shrugged. "Some of it, I guess. It's not quite like the movies where everything just goes up in flames you know?"

"We need guaranteed hellfire," Dani said.

They ducked behind the desk, crouching low to avoid the grinners who were back patrolling the second floor.

"There might be another option," Raven said, "if you want something flammable."

"Yeah?"

Raven's voice shrank to a whisper.

"Remember when the fuel started running out a few months back? Well, Em, as savvy as she was God rest her soul, was ahead of the game. She stocked up about a week before all the panic buying started. Thought we might need some juice for the van, especially if all hell broke loose and we had to get out of Dodge in a hurry. Well it's still here. We never touched it. We got a stash of ten and twenty liter jerry cans locked in the office closet."

Dani pushed the sweat-soaked hair off her face.

"Okay. Here's what we're gonna do. I'm going to go downstairs and create feedback hell for the grinners. You wait here till the feedback loop drives them crazy and when you have a chance, and I'm talking about a clean chance, then go. Run. Go get those cans and bring them back here. As many as you can, as fast as you can."

"Then what?"

Dani smiled. "Then you're going to wash that dirty floor downstairs. Give it a damn good soaking."

Raven's eyes lit up. "We're doing this? We're *really* doing this?"

Dani extended her hand out, palm facing the ceiling.

"What?" Raven asked, frowning. "You want me to give you a quarter or something?"

Dani shook her head. "Give me your lighter."

17

Dani sang 'White Riot' all the way downstairs.

The grinners turned their heads away and she sang even louder, pushing them back with her hands and voice, slamming into their soft, spongy bodies in order to clear a path towards the stage. On her journey from the mixing desk to the first floor, which took about a minute and a half, Dani slipped countless times, covering her stage clothes in blood and God knows what else.

She hurried down both upper and lower staircases, almost losing her balance twice thanks to all the gunk she'd acquired on the base of the cube heels. The shoes looked good, but Dani had already decided they had to go. Flats were more practical. Of course, she'd known that before coming out of the green room as Dani Machete, but now she *knew* it. She just wanted to wear them for a while longer.

Before climbing onstage, Dani crossed the dancefloor and closed the battered front door over. There could be no obvious exits available. Afterwards, she ran back to the stage and pushed herself up onto the wooden platform. Made it to the gig at last, she thought. And she *was* singing, currently on her seventeenth (at least) chorus of 'White Riot.'

The audience wasn't quite what she'd been expecting. Still, a gig was a gig.

Dani shielded her eyes from the overhead lights and looked up towards the mixing desk. It was empty. With any luck, Raven was in the office already, pulling the jerry cans out of the closet.

"WHITE RIOT – I WANNA RIOT!"

Dani grabbed the microphone, pulled it off the stand and screamed into it. Her voice expanded across the room, growing a set of fuck you wings that gave her a taste of what it would have felt like had things gone according to plan that night. She narrowed her eyes, imagining that the grinners swaying on the floor were paying customers dancing to the music that she made.

She stopped singing and pointed the microphone at the monitor. This unleashed a vicious barrage of feedback that sounded like an exorcism gone wrong.

The grinners' floppy, ape-like arms swatted the air, trying to push the feedback away like it was something they could touch.

Dani winced at the ferocity of the high-pitched squealing noise. She covered her left ear with her left hand while at the same time, she tilted her head towards the right shoulder, trying to offer the uncovered ear at least some protection.

She glanced up at the sound desk. Nothing.

After a tortuous minute, she had to pull the mic away from the monitor. Dani staggered backwards, her head OD'ing with echo screech. It was like being drunk, but not good drunk. Definitely not good drunk.

The grinners relaxed as if they'd been released by a

spell. A bald-headed grinner, built like a weightlifter, began to walk towards the stage.

"*munnneee,*" he said, reaching up for Dani like a rabid groupie trying to touch his idol.

"Raven!" Dani yelled through the microphone. "Where are you?"

She took a deep breath, like she was about to dive underwater. Then she stabbed the mic towards the monitors again and the Academy screamed.

Dani, whilst trying to make it through that ungodly noise, stared at the blank TV on the wall. The Loop was gone. There were no more reruns, no endless infomercials about the best value skin creams or which online beauty courses were least threatening to the fragile male egos out there in the world. The only thing on screen was a concise strip of text informing viewers that the Loop was down. But Dani didn't need the Loop, old reruns or with brand new uploads, to know what was going on. She didn't want to see thousands of grinners running riot like something out of a 1950s B-movie. People fleeing in terror, their faces all screwed up and ugly crying. Vacated cocoons. Smashed tanks, broken glass on the sidewalk, and white puddles of pus everywhere.

The swirling feedback intensified, dizzying the grinners. But it was also making Dani feel ill.

A sudden thought occurred to her. What if Raven had taken off? What if she'd run out the fire exit, leaving Dani alone in the Academy with all the grinners to herself? And why not? Raven was smart enough to recognize a golden opportunity when she saw one. With Dani downstairs stunning the grinners like this, there was no need for Raven to stick around and risk getting her heart ripped out. It's not like the two women were close friends.

Just hang in there, Dani thought.

She continued to cover her ears as best she could. Wincing, she put the head of the microphone against the metal grille that shielded the monitor speaker. But to Dani's horror, when she looked up the grinners on the dancefloor were no longer swaying back and forth in distress.

They were walking towards the stage. And their grins were back.

"No."

Dani felt crushed at the sight of the grinners on the move again. Were they adapting to the feedback already?

She was forced to pull the mic away from the monitor. The Academy was silent except for the sound of the grinners' naked feet slapping against the floor.

Dani retreated from the edge of the stage. The dizziness was overwhelming and she fell onto her back. The incessant ringing in her head was torture. But that was nothing compared to the disappointment of the grinners adapting so quickly to the feedback. Her great plan was a flop.

She sat up and crawled away, picking up the machete off the floor.

The grinners were now at the edge of the stage, looking up towards the raised platform.

"*furkmeeeer.*"

"*allyooorwawnt.*"

Dani pushed herself back to her feet, her head still swimming in feedback. She felt like throwing up again.

More of those slow, dragging footsteps approached the stage. Others were coming from the stairs on Dani's right. All of them making towards the stage.

Dani pointed the machete at the shadowy figures gathering from all sides, the blade being the last barrier between her and the grinners.

Another glance upstairs at the mixing desk.

Empty.

She's gone. You're alone.

Several of the grinners out front put their bloody hands on the stage. They hesitated, as if unsure of how to climb up. But when the first one figured it out, all the other grinners quickly followed suit, climbing up in the exact same manner as the first one. Dani saw that and wondered if all of these things, these hatchlings, grinners, pod-people, whatevers, were working from the same mind.

"C'mon then," Dani said, turning the machete on all of them.

They plodded towards her from stage left, stage right, center stage and stage everywhere else. Dani saw the front door in the distance. If she could open up another channel, just like last times, she could make a run for it and get out.

"C'mon," she hissed.

She heard a strange splashing noise. Looking up, Dani saw a flood of rain pouring down to the first floor from the mixing desk.

It was Raven.

The bartender was back, leaning over the chrome barrier and spilling out the contents of a large jerry can onto the dancefloor. The liquid gushed downwards, showering the grinners still on the main floor. They didn't appear to register the soaking, such was their focus on getting to Dani.

"Yes!" Dani roared, clenching her fist, waving it at Raven. "Hurry up."

Dani was surrounded by grinners again. Unlike on the second floor however, she didn't have much space to move around this time. This was shaping up to be more of a fighting-inside-a-phone-booth type of battle. Those weren't good odds for Dani.

Raven continued to dump the fuel, tossing the empties over her shoulder. "Nearly there! What happened to the feedback?"

Dani shook her head. "Fuckers have adapted. Just hurry it up will you?"

She rushed forward, slashing at the frontline with the machete. It was a pre-emptive attack, trying to discourage them from thinking she was an easy target. There was no skill or grace in Dani's technique. She was a human storm, eating up everything in her path or at least trying to.

A tall, emaciated-looking woman grabbed Dani's arm. The grinner tried to pull Dani towards her, to reel her in closer. Dani, instead of resisting, went with the flow. As she was pulled closer to the leering grinner, Dani dropped down onto one knee, dodging a swift stab from the woman's dagger-knuckles. Dani felt the machete's hilt loosen in her grasp. After securing her grip, she lashed out, slicing the woman's snapping fingers with such force that two of them were left hanging on by fleshy threads.

Dani was back her feet, brandishing the machete in her right hand and trying to make space for herself on the crowded stage. She knew she couldn't stay up there for long. If they rushed her, which hadn't happened yet, it was over. A boy, no more than ten years old with long, rope-like blond hair, charged at her. He was fast – the fastest one she'd encountered yet and he bolted across the stage in the blink of an eye.

"*muneeeeee.*"

Dani used her long legs to kick him back out of range. The boy was knocked off balance and as he staggered to the side, Dani saw the narrow opening he'd created on his way towards her. It wasn't much, but it was most likely the best chance she was going to get.

"DONE!" Raven yelled. "I'm done!"

Upon hearing Raven's voice, Dani threw herself into the thinning channel that had opened up in between the grinners. She didn't think it over. Didn't debate the pros and cons. She just ran, slashing at anything that came too close, be it arms, legs or snapping crab-like fingers.

She jumped offstage, landing badly on a floor that was covered in blood and gasoline. Dani's left foot twisted on the slippery surface and she went down, crying out both because of the pain and the fact that she was practically swimming in a puddle of her ex-husband's blood.

On the brink of exhaustion, she pushed herself onto her hands and knees and then climbed back to her feet. Dani hurried towards the bar, dragging her leg behind her as she crossed the dancefloor. She avoided the gasoline spill as best she could without taking any long detours.

She heard the grinners jumping off the edge of the stage. There was a muddy, wet thump as their feet hit the floor. Sounded like they were landing in a paddling pool.

Dani reached the bar and with the last of her strength, climbed up onto the countertop. She immediately kicked off her shoes, both because they'd been a disaster and also because they were covered in blood and maybe even a little gas. But she was glad at least, that she hadn't gotten any gas on her bare feet.

She grabbed a bar towel off the counter, wrapping it around her hand just in case there was any fuel on her skin. Dani debated taking off her pants too, but there was no time. If she went up in flames, so be it. As long as the grinners did too.

She pulled Raven's Zippo from her back pocket, watching the grinners as they slipped on the wet, sticky floor. Unfortunately for Dani, they always got up again, albeit with a little more gasoline stuck to their skin.

She flipped the Zippo open. She held it aloft and her thumb struck the flint wheel. There was a brief spark and a tall blue flame shot up as if reaching for the sky.

The flame withered and died.

"No."

Dani, telling herself not to panic, struck the wheel again.

"Work goddammit!"

The Zippo coughed up another feeble spark. Third time around, not even that.

"Do it Dani!" Raven called out from above. Dani looked up at the roof of the bar. She couldn't see Raven but she imagined the bartender leaning over the desk, desperately waiting to see the venue go up in flames so she could start making a run towards the fire exit. "Do it. They're fucking coming straight at you!"

"The lighter doesn't work!" Dani roared. "It won't fucking light."

A pause.

"Matches!" Raven said. "Behind the bar. Go to the mirror, right under the huge Jack Daniels bottle. You can't miss it. Quick Dani, please!"

Dani looked across the floor. She saw the frontrunners picking up speed, trying to be the first to reach the finish line and win the prize. They'd adjusted their stride as if to avoid slipping on the wet surface.

"Oh shit," Dani said.

She braced herself and hopped off the bar, her leg almost buckling underneath her. A jolt of electricity cannonballed up and down Dani's body. Hang on, she thought.

If the leg gave way now, she was finished.

The Jack Daniels bottle was impossible to miss. It was the size of a small car, almost. Dani caught sight of her reflection in the bar mirror as she limped over to the bottle. She was covered in all kinds of gross shit, but apart from that and the limp, she was doing okay. Being alive, that was okay wasn't it? Behind her reflection, Dani saw the grinner army crossing the slippery battleground. Some of them looked even worse than her.

She looked around for the matches. There were keys, cards, tacky coasters and finally – bingo – a large pack of Diamond matches on the edge of the back counter. Dani scooped up the Diamonds and limped back over to the other side of the bar.

She climbed onto the countertop, striking a match. Thank Christ, they worked. Dani's hand was steady as she held the tiny flame aloft. Pain, exhaustion and all other sensations drifted to the back of her mind. She watched the sea of grinners skating along the dancefloor and Dani remembered, at the worst possible time she noted, that they'd been people once. Mothers. Fathers. Brothers. Sisters. And those people were still in there somewhere, their souls trapped.

Maybe this would free them.

Dani dropped the match onto the floor and felt the rush of hot air inside the Academy. Jumping off the countertop, she took cover behind the bar as she heard a deep thudding noise behind her, followed by the muffled roar of igniting gasoline.

She poked her head above the counter. Dani saw the grinners burning, all of them wearing a coat of orange flames. They burned like scarecrows, still and silent, although a few were still trying to reach the bar. Some of them even grinned through the scent of burning flesh and kept their arms outstretched. Some called to Dani, their words choked in fire. Eventually these grinners, like all the others, toppled over in a black and charred mess on the floor.

The smoke alarm inside the Academy was ringing.

Dani picked herself up off the floor and staggered towards the door. She felt hot and heavy, overcome with exhaustion and heat. With any luck, Raven was outside already.

She fell against the door, coughing, her fingers grasping at the handle. Behind her, the fire raged, spreading to the second floor. It would eventually find its way to the third and in the end, the Academy would be chewed up and spat out along with everything else in civilization. Memories would live on, only as long as survivors like Dani and Raven lived on.

Dani looked up towards the green room. She barely had the energy left to blow a kiss for her sister.

And there was the Fender too, still intact and plugged into the amp.

Waste of a good instrument, Dani thought.

She pulled the door open and looked outside onto a New York that was far different from the one she'd left behind earlier that day. The streets, as expected, were full of death and grinners. Heavy smoke drifted across the burning city like a monstrous fog, but despite this, the air smelled fresh to Dani, fresher and cleaner than it had smelled for a long time.

THE END

OTHER BOOKS BY MARK GILLESPIE

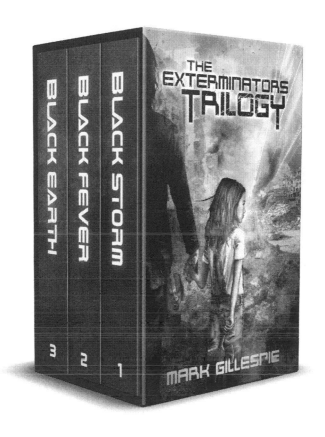

'A pulse-pounding post-apocalyptic horror series.'

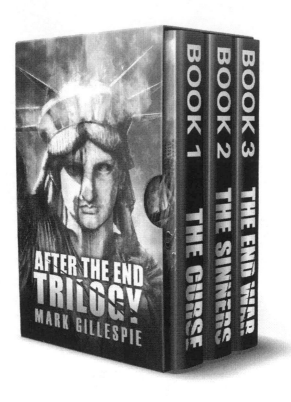

After the End Trilogy (Complete Box Set)
'These are the best of the genre.' - Kindle Reviewer.

'Civic terror, apocalypse, gangs, horror, complete decline of civilization...read it and weep!' - Mallory A. Haws

The Future of London (Books 1-5)

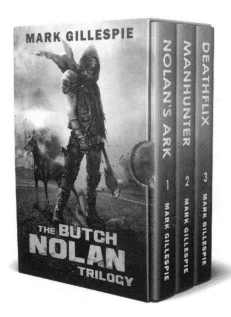

Butch Nolan wants revenge. And not even the end of the world will get in his way.

The Complete Butch Nolan Trilogy

'Stories you won't want to put down!'

Five first in series post-apocalyptic and dystopian books...

Apocalypse No.1

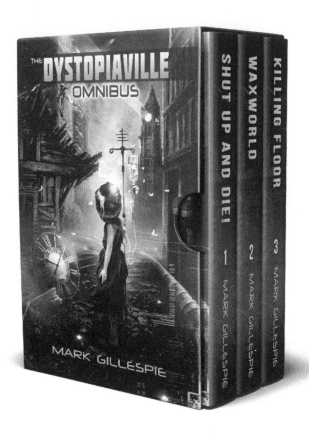

The Dystopiaville Omnibus: 'Think Twilight Zone or Black Mirror, but with books...'

THE BUTCH NOLAN SERIES

Nolan's Ark (Butch Nolan #1)

ManHunter (Butch Nolan #2)

Deathflix (Butch Nolan #3)

Mad Max meets John Wick meets Clint Eastwood's spaghetti westerns in this rollercoaster ride of a post-apocalyptic action thriller...

AFTER THE END TRILOGY

The Curse (After the End #1)

The Sinners (After the End #2)

The End War (After the End #3)

Complete Box Set

"A post-apocalyptic New York run by women...what could go wrong?

Margaret Atwood would be proud."

THE FUTURE OF LONDON

L-2011 (Future of London #1)

Mr Apocalypse (Future of London #2)

Ghosts of London (Future of London #3)

Sleeping Giants (Future of London #4)

Kojiro vs. The Vampire People (Future of London #5)

The Future of London Box Set (Books 1-3)

The Future of London Box Set (Books 1-5)

"Modern dystopian at its very best." - Kirsten McKenzie, author of Painted.

THE EXTERMINATORS TRILOGY

Black Storm

(The Exterminators #1)

Black Fever

(The Exterminators #2)

Black Earth

(The Exterminators #3)

"Part-horror, part post-apocalypse...all brilliant."

DYSTOPIAVILLE

Is this fiction? Or is it the future?

Shut Up and Die!

WaxWorld

Killing Floor

All Dystopiaville books are stand-alone novels/novellas that can be read in any order.

GRIMLOG (TALES OF TERROR)

Apex Predators

Air Nosferatu

Rock Devil

"What's not to like about zombies and sharks, or zombie sharks?" -
CJ (5 stars)

"Brilliantly fast-paced horror that was unputdownable." -
Chantelle Atkins (5 stars)

JOIN THE READER LIST

If you enjoy what you read here and want to be notified whenever there's a new book out, join the reader list. Just click the link below. It'll only take a minute.

www.markgillespieauthor.com

(The sign up box is on the Home Page)

You can also follow Mark on Bookbub.

WEBSITE/SOCIAL MEDIA

Mark Gillespie's author website
www.markgillespieauthor.com

Mark Gillespie on Facebook
www.facebook.com/markgillespieswritingstuff

Mark Gillespie on Twitter
www.twitter.com/MarkG_Author